Alli looked at hi̶ ̶ ̶ ̶ ̶ ̶hocked
expressi̶

Before Jak̶ ̶ ̶ ̶ ̶ ̶ ̶ ̶ ̶ ̶, she
reached ac̶

"It's okay, sw̶ ̶ ̶ ̶ ̶ wiggled her fingers.
"Come here, ̶ ̶ ̶or."

To Jake's surprise, his son readily went to her.
She sat down, ignoring the mess before her, and
rubbed the boy's back, whispering soothing words
while Jake and everyone else did their best to
wipe up the tea that remained on the table.

The crying soon diminished, and Connor found
his fingers.

"Connor," his mother said beside Alli, "would you
like some of Mimi's banana pudding?"

The kid practically threw himself at her. He had
his daddy's sweet tooth, all right.

Standing, Alli glanced around the table. "If you all
will excuse me, please." With that, she continued
to the back door and disappeared into the house.

But not before Jake realized his mother might be
onto something. Alli would be the perfect nanny.
She loved kids, and more importantly, he knew he
could trust her.

If only she didn't hate him.

Award-winning author **Mindy Obenhaus** lives on a ranch in Texas with her husband, two sassy pups, and countless cattle and deer. She's passionate about touching readers with biblical truths in an entertaining, and sometimes adventurous, manner. When she's not writing, you'll usually find her in the kitchen, spending time with family or roaming the ranch. She'd love to connect with you via her website, mindyobenhaus.com.

Books by Mindy Obenhaus

Love Inspired

Hope Crossing

The Cowgirl's Redemption
A Christmas Bargain
Loving the Rancher's Children

Bliss, Texas

A Father's Promise
A Brother's Promise
A Future to Fight For
Their Yuletide Healing

Rocky Mountain Heroes

Their Ranch Reunion
The Deputy's Holiday Family
Her Colorado Cowboy
Reunited in the Rockies
Her Rocky Mountain Hope

Visit the Author Profile page at LoveInspired.com for more titles.

Loving the Rancher's Children

Mindy Obenhaus

LOVE INSPIRED
INSPIRATIONAL ROMANCE

If you purchased this book without a cover you should be aware that this book is stolen property. It was reported as "unsold and destroyed" to the publisher, and neither the author nor the publisher has received any payment for this "stripped book."

LOVE INSPIRED®
INSPIRATIONAL ROMANCE

Recycling programs
for this product may
not exist in your area.

ISBN-13: 978-1-335-58576-9

Loving the Rancher's Children

Copyright © 2023 by Melinda Obenhaus

All rights reserved. No part of this book may be used or reproduced in any manner whatsoever without written permission except in the case of brief quotations embodied in critical articles and reviews.

This is a work of fiction. Names, characters, places and incidents are either the product of the author's imagination or are used fictitiously. Any resemblance to actual persons, living or dead, businesses, companies, events or locales is entirely coincidental.

For questions and comments about the quality of this book, please contact us at CustomerService@Harlequin.com.

Love Inspired
22 Adelaide St. West, 41st Floor
Toronto, Ontario M5H 4E3, Canada
www.LoveInspired.com

Printed in U.S.A.

My grace is sufficient for thee:
for my strength is made perfect in weakness.
—*2 Corinthians* 12:9

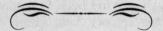

For Your Glory, Lord

Acknowledgments

Many thanks to Cheryl Leyendecker,
Debbie Gregory, Amy Haysler and
Danielle Tanner for enduring my countless
questions and helping me bring this story to life.
Love you all! And to my wonderful husband, who is
the best support system this author could ask for.
I love you more than words can express.

Chapter One

Alli Krenek hadn't felt this well rested in ages.

Being back in the country, away from the 24/7 noise that seemed to abound in the city, was obviously agreeing with her. But then, she'd come home to her father's ranch countless times since moving to Austin a dozen years ago and had never slept this well.

Perhaps it was seeing her father so happy. He'd remarried ten months ago, and that had brought him a contentment he'd been missing since losing her mother to cancer five years ago.

Staring at her reflection in the bathroom mirror, Alli threaded a faux diamond stud into each earlobe, well aware it was neither of those things. Instead, after eight years with Child Protective Services, she could finally sleep easy knowing that no one was looking to her for guidance, protection or the preservation of their family. Friday a week ago had been her last day. And at the urging of her father and stepmom, she'd given up her tiny apartment in Austin and come home to reconnect with her roots while she worked toward a new career as a teacher.

A career she prayed would help her finally move past the loss of four-year-old Lacy Hayes.

Shaking off the unwanted thought, Alli exited the tiny bathroom to make the full-size bed in what had once been her father's man cave over the detached garage. Since he rarely used it anymore, her stepmom, Francie, had decided to reclaim the space already equipped with a bathroom and kitchenette to use for guests.

Truth be known, it was nicer than the studio apartment Alli had paid way too much for in downtown Austin. With vinyl plank flooring, white cabinetry, a cozy sitting area and sleeping alcove, her new digs exuded that whole farmhouse vibe. And since it was separate from the house, both she and the newlyweds enjoyed a measure of privacy.

After a parting glance at her reflection in the cheval mirror beside the door, she smoothed a hand over her pale blue cotton dress and made her way outside. The early April sun warmed her skin, and birdsong filled the air as she continued down the steps and toward the house.

Inside the seventies-era ranch-style house, the aromas of coffee and bacon mingled with the brisket Francie had put in the oven last night, awakening Alli's appetite as she entered the newly renovated kitchen. Yes, Francie had breathed new life into just about everything around here. Not the least of which was Alli's father. His playful side had been on full display since Alli arrived Monday. She'd missed that and feared it had died forever right along with her mother.

"Mornin', Alli Cat." Daddy looked up from his eggs, his light brown hair with whispers of gray still damp from his shower.

"Morning, Alli." Francie, a sixtysomething blonde Alli had known all her life, who was also widowed, smiled beside him, a slice of whole wheat toast topped with butter and jam in her hand.

"Good morning." Alli paused beside the rustic wood table in front of the bay window that overlooked the backyard to kiss her father's clean-shaven cheek. How she loved this man. For as long as Alli could remember, Bill Krenek had been her hero. A role no other man had been able to fill.

"You're lookin' mighty pretty today." His pale blue-green eyes met hers. "Looks like I'll have my work cut out for me, fending off all those single fellas at church."

"All?" Lifting a brow, Alli continued to the coffeepot beside the farmhouse sink on the peninsula that overlooked the freshly painted family room. "Hope Crossing has a population of less than four hundred." She snagged a mug from the cupboard. "So *all* is relative." After pouring her second cup of the day—the first having come from the Keurig in her apartment—she moved to the stainless-steel refrigerator for some creamer.

"You might be surprised," her father said. "There are enough that they've formed a single adult Sunday school class."

Mug in hand, she joined them at the table, taking the seat across from her father. "That'll be nice." Until now, the only singles class was labeled College and Career. "Now I won't have to go to the married adult class with you t—I mean, you won't have to have me tagging along with you." The only thing worse than being in a class with college-age kids was being in a class with two lovestruck sixtysomethings.

"I believe Jake Walker is in that class." Daddy scooped up the last of his eggs, pushing the little bits onto his fork with what remained of his bacon. "You know he's widowed, right?"

"Yes, you've pointed that out a time or two." More like ten or twenty.

There was a time when Alli and Jake had been best friends. Almost from the cradle. His dad owned the adjoining ranch, so they were always together, either goofing off or helping their fathers work cattle. They were both horsemen and challenged each other to hone their cutting skills when they'd sort cattle. But just when she thought they were on the verge of becoming more, Jake broke her heart. And things had been different ever since.

Francie's phone buzzed beside her plate. She glanced at the screen, her brow puckering. "Dottie Rodgers? I wonder why she's calling." She tapped the screen and placed the phone to her ear. "Hello."

Alli savored a couple sips of coffee before fixing her own slice of toast with peanut butter.

"Sure, I'd be happy to help," she heard Francie say. "Maybe Alli would like to join me."

She turned at the mention of her name.

"On second thought, she might prefer to attend Sunday school, this being her first week back and all." Francie twisted to face her. "Hold on a sec, Dottie." Looking at Alli, Francie said, "One of the nursery workers is under the weather, so Dottie asked me to cover the Sunday school hour. I could probably use the help if you're interested. If not, I'll ask Gloriana." She was Francie's daughter.

Hmm…playing with babies and toddlers or spending an hour in a small classroom with Jake Walker? "I'd be happy to help." Besides, it would do her heart good to interact with children whose lives remained untouched by the ugliness of this world.

Once she'd finished her toast and a slice of bacon, they loaded into Francie's Tahoe and headed off for Hope Crossing Bible Church. The very one where Alli's parents had dedicated her to the Lord as an infant and where she'd been baptized as a teenager. Sadly, her view of life had been jaded since then. She'd witnessed things that sometimes had her questioning why God allowed them, especially to children.

The morning air was laced with the aroma of spring flowers as they made their way from the parking lot to the steepled, beige brick building. And within minutes they were surrounded by Francie's two children and their families.

Hawkins Prescott, her oldest, was slated to marry Annalise Grant in just a matter of weeks and would be an instant father to her adorable twenty-two-month-old daughter, Olivia. Meanwhile, Francie's daughter, Gloriana, had married Justin Broussard last fall. They had a fifteen-year-old daughter, Kyleigh, and were expecting a baby sometime this summer. Altogether, the whole lot of them took up an entire pew—something Alli, an only child, appreciated more than one might imagine.

She'd just made herself comfortable between Francie and Gloriana when she saw Jake Walker moving past the beautiful stained-glass windows on the opposite side of the sanctuary. Though she tried not to stare, she couldn't help noticing his thick, sandy brown hair was a little longer than it had been in high school and parted slightly off center. And with his shirt tucked in, it was obvious he was as lean as ever.

He slipped into the cushioned wood pew beside his mother, doing a double take when he spotted Alli. And his gaze seemed to be trained on her for the rest of the service. At least until the pastor began his sermon.

So Alli was pleased when Francie suggested they slip out during the closing prayer and go on to the nursery.

"This isn't at all like I remember." Alli took in the brightly colored space with a Noah's ark theme, recalling the bland pastel green walls when she used to help out there in high school.

"Isn't it fun?" Francie closed the half door behind them to prevent any escapees. "They redid things a couple of years ago."

Dottie Rodgers approached, her smile wide, and gave Alli a hug. "Sweet thing, I believe you get prettier every time I see you." The woman with short, silver hair had been Alli's Sunday school teacher all the way through high school. Back when all the other girls seemed to be blossoming and Alli was still desperately awaiting her turn.

"It's good to see you again," Alli said as Dottie released her.

Looking to Francie and back, Dottie said, "I put name tags on the children's backs, so y'all will know who's who." Dottie opened a childproofed cupboard and retrieved her purse. "And everyone has either pottied or been changed in the last fifteen minutes so you should be good for a while."

"Dottie, you are nothing if not efficient." A smiling Francie tucked her blond bob behind her ear before picking up her soon-to-be granddaughter, Olivia.

"Thank you both for stepping in."

Francie waved her off. "The pleasure is ours."

As Dottie departed, Alli eyed the other five kiddos. The littlest looked to be around nine months and she simply sat atop the animal-themed rug, wide-eyed, observing Tori Stallings's four-year-old son, Aiden, and a girl who looked to be around the same age, as they engaged in a race between his dinosaur and her unicorn.

"That's *mine*," another boy insisted somewhere behind her.

Alli turned toward the colorful cubbies lining the far wall as one boy snatched something from a smaller boy.

The little one's face reddened, his eyes shimmering. *Uh-oh.*

She hurried toward them. "Hey, guys." She knelt to their level. "What seems to be the problem?"

The auburn-haired boy she placed somewhere around three-and-a-half clutched the action figure and glared at the littler boy. "He stole my toy."

Alli looked at the toddler with white-blond hair and innocent blue-gray eyes as he shoved his middle and index fingers into his mouth and began sucking. Poor little guy probably had no idea he'd *stolen* the toy, as the other boy suggested.

"Let's see if we can find you a different toy." Standing, she held out her hand as the older boy—Finn, according to Dotty's strip of tape—scurried away.

When the toddler took hold, she noted the tag on his back. "What do you like to play with, Connor?"

Surprisingly, he bypassed the toys and tugged her toward the bookshelf. A boy after her own heart.

Again, she knelt. "Which book would you like to read?"

He tentatively touched a couple of board books before another child said, "That one's his favorite."

Turning, Alli smiled at the girl with the unicorn, immediately noticing the resemblance. "Is this your brother?"

"Uh-huh." The girl with blonde curls that fell to the

middle of her back nodded emphatically. "His name is Connor. He's two-and-a-half. I'm Maddy, and I'm four." She held up as many fingers.

"It's nice to meet you, Maddy. I'm Miss Alli."

Connor took hold of the book his sister had pointed out and handed it to Alli, his gaze hopeful.

"Will you read it to us?"

Looking into Maddy's pleading blue eyes, Alli smiled. Reading to children was one of her favorite things ever. "Of course."

Dressed in a cap-sleeved chambray dress adorned with white stars, Maddy hurried toward one of two rocking chairs, her brown cowboy boots echoing against the tile floor. "Guys, Miss Alli is gonna read to us."

Alli eased into the rocking chair, smiling when the other kids plopped down on the rug and fixed their gazes on her. She loved watching the children's faces as she made the stories come to life. Back in Austin, she often read at one of the women's shelters. Watching the kids' faces transform as they forgot their worries and became engrossed in whatever tale she was reading always made her smile.

Francie settled into the chair opposite and began rocking Olivia. And as Alli opened the board book, Connor crawled into her lap.

"Are you ready?"

"Yeah!" a couple of the kids cheered, while the others nodded.

"Brown bear, brown bear, *what* do you see?" She changed her voice for each of the different animals, giving them a distinct personality. The kids got a kick out of it. Little Connor had the most adorable belly laugh.

When she finished, another child asked her to read

their favorite book. And then another. By the time she finished, parents were arriving.

Francie greeted Finn's mom and dad while Alli returned all the books to the shelf.

"Mama, Miss Alli read to us," said Aiden when his mother arrived. Tori and Alli had known each other since elementary school, so, since Tori was a teacher, Alli had been in touch with her regarding some of the requirements Alli would need to fulfill for her teaching certification.

"Wow!" Tori's eyes were wide. "I've never seen him so excited about reading."

"She did voices and everything," he said.

Tori perched a hand on her hip as she addressed her son. "I do voices all the time."

He poked a thumb in Alli's direction. "Miss Alli's are better." He looked up at her. "Will you be here next week?"

His question warmed Alli's heart. "I don't think so, but perhaps I can come back another time."

While Francie chatted with baby Shiloh's parents, Alli began picking up toys. Until Connor came alongside her, wanting to be held.

Happy to indulge in some more snuggles, she lifted him into her arms. And when he laid his head on her shoulder, she smoothed a hand over his back, savoring the scents of baby shampoo and fish crackers.

"Daddy!" At Maddy's cheer, Alli turned, her heart dropping like a lead weight.

"There's my girl." Jake Walker leaned over the half door and lifted the beautiful child into his arms. "Did you have fun?"

Maddy nodded emphatically before squeezing her daddy's neck. "We had a new teacher today."

"You did?" Jake's gray eyes found Alli then.

Her heart all but stopped. For a moment, she was seventeen again and smitten with the boy next door. The boy who'd captured her heart and then tossed it aside, right along with their friendship.

Then she heard Maddy say, "Maybe she could be our new nanny, Daddy. Please, please, please?"

Jake stood there holding his daughter, feeling every bit as uncomfortable as Alli looked. He'd seen her in church. Yet while he longed to talk to her, he knew his efforts would prove futile, the way they had every other time he'd approached her over the past seventeen years. The only conversation they'd had in recent history was when she extended her condolences after his wife's passing sixteen months ago.

He certainly hadn't expected to find Alli in the nursery, though. And standing this close, her brilliant blue eyes boring into him while her chocolate brown waves tumbled past her shoulders, had rendered him speechless. Man, she was pretty.

Alli Krenek may have been a late bloomer, but she seemed to get more beautiful each and every time he saw her. Throw in the way Connor was nestled against her shoulder and Jake's heart was about to beat right out of his chest.

Forcing himself to look away, he said, "Settle down, Maddy. Miss Alli is only here to visit her father for a few days." Besides, no matter how much he needed a nanny, Alli would probably rather have a bad case of poison ivy than work for him.

Bill rounded the corner then. "Naw, she's stickin' around for a while this time." Seriously? And Jake was just now finding out? He thought Bill was his friend. A little warning would've been nice.

The news had a splinter of something he wasn't sure he wanted to name—hope, excitement…terror—ricocheting through him. "She—"

"Alli, my darlin'." His mother, Joanna, propelled her petite self between him and Bill, and continued through the doorway to embrace Alli and Connor collectively. "Oh, how I've missed you, sweet girl."

Alli's smile was genuine as she hugged his mother back, albeit with one arm. The two of them had always had a special relationship. Alli was like the daughter Mom never had. And while Jake was glad it hadn't been a casualty of his youthful foolishness, he was also a little jealous of the bond they still shared.

Releasing Alli, his mother tucked her own shoulder-length brown curls behind one ear, practically beaming. "Is it true you're going to be staying in Hope Crossing?"

Alli nodded. "While I work toward getting my teaching certificate. Then we'll see where I end up."

So it really was true? Why hadn't Bill said anything before now? Unless someone had asked him not to.

"Daddy?" Still in his arms, Maddy wiggled. "I want down."

"Oh, sorry, Madikins." He set her booted feet on the light gray linoleum, his gaze still fixed on Alli. She was the best friend he'd ever had. Way back when, she'd known him inside and out. His likes, dislikes. His strengths and flaws. With her, he could be himself. And she was always there for him. Until he ruined everything.

Not once had he regretted asking Alli out on that date. Though he wished he'd been man enough to ignore his buddies and follow his heart instead of their ridiculous whims. To this day, it still wrecked him, knowing he'd hurt Alli. One stupid move had cost him his best friend and, if he were honest, a few what-could've-beens. And now that he'd become personally acquainted with betrayal's sting, he felt even worse.

"Joanna?" Francie's voice dragged him from the depths of regret. "Why don't you, Jake and the kids join us for Sunday dinner? You know I always have more than enough food."

His mother pressed her coral lips together for a moment before lifting a brow. "Are you sure, Francie? Your group has grown considerably this past year."

"I know! Isn't it wonderful?" The woman with the blond bob beamed. "Who cares if I have fewer left-overs?"

While the two women shared a laugh, Alli's wary gaze briefly slid to his. Still holding Connor, she stepped closer, until only the door separated them.

"Are you ready to go see your daddy?"

Connor lifted his head, smiling around those two fingers that always seemed to be in his mouth, though he didn't appear to be in any big hurry to bid Alli farewell.

"Aw, would you look at that." His mother moved beside Alli, her smile wide as she smoothed a hand over Connor's hair. "It appears there's another Walker boy who's smitten with you, Alli."

Pink bloomed on Alli's cheeks while Jake wished he could disappear into the floor.

Clueless as to how her statement had impacted them, his mother glanced his way. "What do you say, Jakey? You up for one of Francie's delectable Sunday dinners?"

Francie Krenek, formerly Prescott, was one of the best cooks in Hope Crossing. One would have to be off his rocker to turn down one of her meals. So why was Jake contemplating doing just that?

Because Francie now lived in Bill's house, where Alli was staying.

"Can we, Daddy?" Maddy bounced beside him, her little hands clasped in a pleading manner. "Will Miss Alli be there?"

"Yes, I'm sure she will be." And she probably wasn't too thrilled with Francie's offer, so the least he could do was make things easy on her. "However, your brother will be ready for a nap soon."

"No nap." Connor's unhappy tone had Jake looking over the half door to see his son scowling at him.

Francie scurried about the room, picking up toys. "I don't know about everyone else, but I want to hear *all* about this cruise you're going on, Joanna. Who knows?" She paused, a toy dinosaur in her hand. "Maybe one of these days I can talk Bill into taking me on one."

The man harrumphed beside Jake, then moved out of the way as Francie's son, Hawkins, appeared with his fiancée.

"Sorry we're late." Annalise, a bubbly blonde who owned the Hope Crossing Christmas Tree Farm, continued through the door. "Our class was a *little* chatty today." She stooped to pick up her daughter, who wasn't quite two yet, and peppered her with kisses, much to the child's delight.

"You're fine, dear," said Francie. "We've been busy chatting ourselves. I'm trying to talk Joanna and Jake into joining us for dinner."

"That'd be great. Olivia would love having some friends her size for a change."

Alli lifted those incredible blue eyes to Jake's. "It's a losing battle. You may as well just come on."

Unlike when they were younger, he couldn't get a good read on her. Did she want him to come or was she merely giving him permission? He didn't want her to be uncomfortable.

"Yeah, Daddy." Maddy latched on to his leg and peered up at him. "C'mon."

Jake thought for a moment. Was God providing him with the opportunity he'd long hoped for? Though just the thought of having a real conversation with Alli was as terrifying as it was exciting.

Peering down at his daughter, he said, "Alright. We can go."

Once the classroom was returned to order, they all piled into their respective vehicles and caravanned to Bill and Francie's, where slow-cooked beef brisket awaited, along with more sides than Jake could count.

Since the weather was only a hair shy of perfect with temperatures in the midseventies and the humidity virtually nonexistent, they ate on the covered patio overlooking the backyard that was home to an impressive oak tree and extensive vegetable and flower gardens, along with an ornate white chicken coop. Two wooden picnic tables had been pushed together to create one long table that could accommodate everyone.

"I'm just so tickled to have you back for a while." His mother sat beside Alli, with Maddy tucked in between them. "We need to get together one day soon."

"I'd like that, Joanna." Alli cut a piece of meat. "Maybe we can do lunch sometime."

"Now you're talking." His mother gathered the last of her broccoli salad onto her fork. "So you mentioned teaching. Does that mean you're no longer with CPS?"

Across the table from them, Jake helped Connor with his macaroni and cheese, hoping to appear more engrossed in his son than their conversation, despite hanging on their every word.

"Correct. I'm hoping to teach preschool or early elementary."

Of course she was. Alli had always loved children. She'd once told him she wanted six of her own. Something that would give any teenage boy pause.

Francie pushed through the screen door, holding a large glass bowl. "Who's ready for some banana pudding?" After settling between his mother and Bill, she began scooping the dessert into small disposable bowls. "So tell me about this cruise, Joanna."

"Well." Moving her plate aside, Mom dabbed the corners of her mouth with her napkin. "We set sail out of Vancouver on a Sunday and then spend the next eight days hopping up the coast of Alaska."

Jake offered Connor a bite of the dessert Francie had handed him, enjoying the anticipation in his mother's voice and the sparkle in her eyes as she went on about the details of her upcoming trip. He wanted her to enjoy life instead of being tied down to his children. She'd just begun to find her way without his father when Jake's wife, Bethany, died unexpectedly. Yet she stepped right in to care for Maddy and Connor without ever blinking an eye.

Now, almost a year and a half later, it was time for Jake to move on with his life and for his mother to reclaim hers, starting with that cruise. Even if it meant he had to haul the kids with him while he worked the ranch. Not that he'd get much done.

"That sounds so exciting." Francie finished passing bowls down the table. "You know Hawkins lived in Alaska for several years."

At the far end of the table, Francie's eldest held Olivia

in his lap. "Joanna, you won't be disappointed. Alaska has so much to offer. And Denali is spectacular."

"I can hardly wait. I've always wanted to experience Alaska, so I figure if I'm going to do it, I may as well do it up right."

Dipping a spoon into his dessert, Hawkins nodded. "I look forward to hearing what you think."

"Who's going with you, again?" With everyone else served, Francie settled in with her own helping of the delicious dessert.

"Ginny Loftus. Used to be Ginny Franklin." His mother glanced at Francie. "She lives in Houston now, but she lost her husband right about the same time my Ralph passed away."

That was when Jake decided to turn in his badge at the Houston Police Department and return to Hope Crossing to take over the ranch. Maddy wasn't even six months old, and Bethany had gone on and on about how she wanted her children to be raised in the country the way he'd been. He never would've guessed that only a couple years later, his wife would be singing a very different tune.

Francie suddenly appeared perplexed. "Who's going to watch Maddy and Connor while you're gone?"

Jake wiped Connor's hands. "The plan has always been for me to hire a nanny." A process he would have started even sooner had his mother not been so insistent that the kids needed time to adjust to their mother being gone before bringing in a stranger. Now they'd all have to adjust again. He just prayed that whoever he hired would be trustworthy. Thankfully, he still had friends on the force willing to run background checks for him.

"Though finding the right person has proven to be a little more challenging out here in the boonies," he continued. "As you know, we ranchers don't necessarily have nine-to-five jobs."

His mother started to take another bite of her pudding then lowered her spoon, her gaze bobbing from Alli to Jake and back. "I can't believe I didn't think of this before." She rested her spoon in her bowl. "Alli, dear, you just might be the answer to our prayers."

Alli's eyes rounded. "How so?"

"You said yourself you want to work with kids. What if you were to nanny for Maddy and Connor? Even if it's only temporary."

Jake couldn't help noticing Alli's dismayed expression. As though she found the thought of working for him repulsive.

"I—" Alli started.

"No, Mom."

Everyone looked at Jake.

"Have you forgotten that we have interviews scheduled for tomorrow? Besides, you're not being fair to Alli, putting her on the spot like this." His gaze shifted to Alli as Connor reached for Jake's red plastic cup. "I'm sor—"

The cup toppled before Jake could take hold of it, sending tea and ice cubes racing across the table, straight toward Alli.

With a gasp, she shot to her feet, staring at the tea-soaked spot on her dress.

While both Francie and his mother scrambled to sop up the mess, Connor let out a loud wail and burst into tears.

Alli looked from her dress to his son, her shocked expression softening. Before Jake realized what was happening, she reached across the table.

"It's okay, sweet boy." She wiggled her fingers. "Come here, Connor."

To Jake's surprise, his son readily went to her. She sat down, ignoring the mess before her, and rubbed the boy's back, whispering soothing words while Jake and everyone else did their best to wipe up the tea that remained on the table.

The crying soon diminished, and Connor found his fingers.

"Connor," his mother said beside Alli, "would you like some of Mimi's banana pudding?"

The kid practically threw himself at her. He had his daddy's sweet tooth, all right.

Standing, Alli glanced around the table. "If you all will excuse me, please." With that, she continued to the back door and disappeared into the house.

But not before Jake realized his mother might be on to something. Alli would be the perfect nanny. She loved kids and, more importantly, he knew he could trust her.

If only she didn't hate him.

Chapter Two

Alli hurried up the steps to her apartment, eager to change out of her wet clothes. And even more desperate to escape the awkward situation downstairs.

She knew Joanna was simply trying to help, but when she suggested Alli care for Jake's children, Alli had been ready to turn tail and run. Yet, while Connor had presented her with the perfect opportunity to do just that, she couldn't bring herself to abandon the little guy when it was her reaction that'd made him cry.

She pushed open the door, tossing it closed behind her as she made a beeline for the closet. In a matter of minutes, she'd traded her dress and strappy sandals for a pair of olive green shorts, a plain white T-shirt and flip-flops. After putting the dress in the bathroom sink with some cold water and sending up a prayer that the tea wouldn't leave a stain, she twisted her hair up and affixed it to the back of her head with a clip.

Back in the day, get-togethers with the Walkers and the Prescotts had been a common occurrence. And Alli, Jake, Gloriana and Hawkins had always enjoyed each other's company. Whether they were pitching washers, riding horses, fishing or running off to a nearby swimming hole, things had always been easy, comfortable, despite the major crush she'd had on Jake.

Then, in the spring of her junior year—his senior year—he'd asked her out on a date. Dinner and a movie, he'd said. She was so excited that she spent her hard-earned money on a cute pink sundress that was much more feminine than the jeans and T-shirt Jake was used to seeing her wear. She'd even put on makeup. And then he never showed up.

By the next day, her disappointment had been over-shadowed by anger. She went to his house, spitting mad, and called him out right in front of his friends who were there. She'd never seen his face so ruddy. Yet he still had the nerve to tell her he'd only been joking about them going out. That he didn't think she'd take him seriously.

Glimpsing herself in the mirror now, she shook her head. Taking care of Maddy and Connor would be the perfect interim job for her. She'd be doing something she loved. And they lived just up the road so it couldn't be more convenient.

That is, if Jake wasn't their father.

She turned out the light and shuffled out of the bath-room, well aware that she was behaving more like an adolescent than an adult, holding a grudge over some-thing that happened seventeen years ago. Both she and Jake had moved on with their lives. But ever since her fiancé broke things off a week before they were sup-posed to wed last year, those old feelings of insecurity and unworthiness had resurfaced. And while the ache had subsided, she still couldn't help wondering what was wrong with her.

With a sigh, she snagged a water bottle from the small refrigerator before flopping down in one of two easy chairs and propping her feet on the square, wooden coffee table. She should probably go back downstairs and see everyone off. She'd hate for them to think her rude.

As she stood, though, there was a knock on the door. Probably her father checking on her. Maybe Francie. Or Joanna.

Setting her water on the table, she crossed to the door and peeked through the blinds to see who was on the other side. Then nearly choked when she saw Jake standing there, looking more handsome than a man had a right to.

She sucked in a breath that was anything but calming before opening the door. "Yes?"

"May I come in?"

Oh, how she wanted to say no. She just couldn't bring herself to do it.

Stepping aside, she motioned for him to enter, then closed the door behind him.

"Wow." He took in the space. "This place looks nothing at all like I remember." As teenagers, they used to come up here and play pool or darts.

She crossed her arms over her chest, managing a smile. "Pretty crazy, huh?"

"In a good way, though. This is nice." His gray eyes captured hers. "Gives you some privacy, too."

Nodding, she watched a wren flit past the window behind the sitting area. A pair of them had been working on a nearby nest and were constantly going back and forth, sometimes pausing on the outside sill to peer at her.

She rubbed her suddenly chilled arms. "I'm guessing you didn't come up here for a tour."

"No." Hands slung low on his dark-wash-denim-clad hips, Jake continued. "I wanted to apologize for my mother. She doesn't always think before she speaks. I'm sorry if she put you in an awkward position down there."

Alli waved him off. "Joanna says whatever's on her mind. But she didn't mean any harm." Unlike her son, whose so-called joke had been downright cruel.

"That's good. I just didn't want you to feel any pressure."

"Nope, I'm good." Still holding herself for fear she'd fall apart, she rocked back on her heels.

"What about your dress? It's not stained, is it? If so, I'm happy to buy you a new one. Or reimburse you. Or whatever."

Her gaze narrowed. Jake was nervous. He'd always prattled on like that when he was uncomfortable.

Just knowing she wasn't the only one had her feeling a little better. "No, it'll be fine." At least, she hoped so since it was one of her favorites. "Is that all you wanted to say?"

He began to pace then. Not that there was much space to do that, especially with his long legs. "Look, since you're going to be here for the foreseeable future, there's something I need to get off my chest."

She watched him, her anxiety heightening. She wasn't in the mood to rehash the past.

Stopping, he raked his fingers through his thick hair, his expression pinched when he looked at her again. "I'm sorry. I behaved like a jerk, messing you over back in high school. And not just in standing you up."

Curiosity had her lifting a brow as he drew in a long breath.

"When I told you it had only been a joke, I lied. The truth is, I was really looking forward to our date. But when my friends learned I'd asked you out, well, they gave me a hard time about it."

"Of course they did." Annoyance had her dropping her arms to her sides. "I wasn't the kind of girl the star football player would date. I was a tomboy. An awkward one at that. They used to make fun of me."

He watched her intently now. "I never saw you that way."

"But you didn't shut them down either."

"And you have no idea how much I've regretted that. Aside from hurting you, I lost my best friend."

Her spine stiffened, her gaze narrowing. "Jake, a real friend wouldn't have cared what anyone else thought or said. A real friend would've stood up for me."

"Wow." The word rushed out on a breath. He sank into the chair she'd vacated only moments ago. Elbows on his thighs, he stared at the floor. "And just when I thought I couldn't feel any worse." After a long, silent moment, he looked up at her, his expression pained. "You're right. I should have done those things." He pushed to his feet. "And I *am* truly sorry." His gaze bore into her. "Despite what you may think, you were my best friend. And I'd like it if we could somehow find our way back to—" His shoulders drooped. "Okay, that's probably asking too much."

"Yep." She shoved her hands into her pockets, trying to appear calm while inside she was anything but. A part of her wanted to rail at him, hurting him the way he'd hurt her, while the other part was best left ignored.

His face contorted. "Do you suppose we could at least carry on a conversation that isn't so…awkward?"

Releasing a breath, she said, "Jake, seventeen years is a long time." She lifted a shoulder. "It's not like we can just pick up where we left off. For starters, I trusted you back then. I can't say that now."

He nodded, his expression grim. "Then I guess I'm

just going to have to earn it again." With that, he whisked past her to pause at the door. "I've missed you, Alli."

As he disappeared outside, Alli realized why she'd never given him the opportunity to apologize before. Because he'd say everything she wanted to hear, and she'd forgive him.

And she'd been absolutely right.

Jake sat at his kitchen table the next afternoon, certain this had to be one of the most difficult things he'd ever done. Harder than apologizing to Alli yesterday. Tougher than facing an ornery bull. More unnerving than burying his wife.

Entrusting the care and well-being of his children to a stranger surpassed each and every one of those things. What if he made a wrong choice? What if these prospective caretakers weren't who they appeared to be? If something happened to Maddy or Connor he'd never survive.

"Each of the two women we interviewed seemed delightful." His mother set two mason jars of iced tea on the farmhouse-style table before settling into the white wooden chair opposite him while Maddy and Connor played on the floor in the adjoining living room, halfheartedly watching the movie they'd insisted he turn on.

Beauty, their massive mastiff, lay nearby, watching over them.

"Of course they did. Everyone puts their best foot forward when interviewing for a job."

Mom sighed, scooped up Beast, a tiny furball of a mutt, and settled him into her lap. "Your days as a police officer have jaded you."

"More like opened my eyes." Growing up in Hope Crossing, he'd lived a rather idyllic life. He couldn't say the same about his time in Houston, not with the things he'd seen.

"Okay, let's try to break it down." Absently stroking Beast's soft fur, Mom eyed the spiral notebook with her notes. "What was your first impression of Ariane?"

He fingered the condensation on his glass. "Young. Attractive. Not as professional as I would've liked."

His mother arched a brow. "She was flirting with you."

"Something like that. Which got my mind going in another direction." He straightened. "I'm a single father. What if someone decided to use that against me?"

"What do you mean?"

"Like accusing me of inappropriate behavior."

"Or looking for a sugar daddy."

The corners of his mouth lifted. "Yeah, like I totally give off that kind of vibe."

"As you always say, Officer Walker, stranger things." She took a long drink. "So what are your thoughts on Kathy?"

"Capable. Down-to-earth. Motherly. The kids seemed to like her, too. But she also made no bones about the fact that she didn't care for the long drive out here."

Mom nodded. "Said it would take too much gas."

Visually monitoring things in the living room, he said, "I mean, I could try to overcome her objection by countering with more money to cover the gas, but I'm already offering to pay as much or more than I can afford just so we'll get some quality candidates."

"Well, a true quality candidate wouldn't care about the money."

"Everyone's got bills to pay, Mom."

She continued to stroke Beast. "Neither of us wants

to settle when it comes to Maddy and Connor, so perhaps we should rethink things."

His gaze cut to his mother. "You're going on that cruise, Mom."

"Yes, you've made that perfectly clear. That's not what I was going to suggest, though."

"Go ahead."

"Kyleigh Broussard is almost sixteen, yet while she may be young, she's very capable and happens to adore children. Annalise has her sit for Olivia quite often."

"She's also in school."

"School will be out by the time I leave for Alaska. You could hire her to take care of the children while I'm gone, then when I return, I'll resume caring for them until we find the perfect candidate."

Jake blew out a breath. While that wasn't necessarily a bad option, he'd hoped his mother would be free to live her own life.

"Of course, there's one more option."

He waited.

"Alli."

"No."

"I don't understand why you're so quick to discount her."

"I'm not discounting her, Mom. She's not even up for consideration."

She studied him. "No one would ever guess the two of you were almost inseparable at one time." Lifting a shoulder, she added, "At one point, I even thought y'all might be on your way to becoming more than friends."

He had, too. Though, he had no one but himself to blame for the demise of their relationship. "Mom, I know how much you love Alli, but you saw how she was yesterday. She could barely stand to be in the same room with me."

"Can't say as I blame her. You broke her heart, Jake."

"I don't know about that, but I sure made her mad." In his mind's eye, he could still see her face that day she showed up here while he was playing basketball with a couple guys whose opinions shouldn't have meant squat to him. Yet he'd lied to her, foolishly believing he'd be able to smooth things over later.

He'd never been more wrong.

Mom cocked her head. "Mind if I ask where you disappeared to after dessert yesterday?"

"I went to Alli's apartment to apologize for you."

"Me?" Indignation straightened her spine. "What did I do?"

"The same thing you're doing right now. Trying to push Alli and me together." He took a drink. "And then I took what might've been my one and only opportunity and apologized for what I did to her back in high school."

A hopeful glint sparked in his mother's brown eyes. "And?"

He shrugged. "She doesn't trust me."

After a silent moment, his mother said, "Since we have to keep lowering our expectations, perhaps you should reconsider day care."

"I called them last week. Both age groups are already full."

"Well, boo." She slumped in her chair. "It appears we've exhausted all of our options, then. That is, unless you want to go with something I suggested. In the meantime, we'll just pray on it and see what God has in store, because while He may not be early, He's never late. He knows what we need. We just need to cling to that and be patient."

Jake knew his mother was right, but at the moment, his hope was on shaky ground.

"I need to make a run to Plowman's for a couple of T-posts." He stood, grabbed his glass and took it to the sink.

"Want to pick up some bacon and milk while you're there?" Mom pushed her chair away from the table. "You're running low on both."

"Anything else?"

Still in his mother's lap, Beast eyed Jake as though he were following the conversation.

"A loaf of bread wouldn't hurt, I suppose. And you can always see what they've got at the bakery."

"Will do." After hugging his children, he continued into the laundry room, snagging his hat from the hook on the wall before heading out the back door where he shoved his socked feet into his dusty old boots.

Then he ambled toward his truck under a cloud-dotted sky, once again filled with appreciation for his mama. Without her, he wasn't sure he would've made it through these last sixteen months. His world had been turned upside down the day Bethany died. Even before the accident. Because that was the same day his wife had informed him she'd found someone else and wanted a divorce.

Mere hours later, Jake received word of her accident and that she'd passed.

How horrible of a person was he that his first thought hadn't been about his kids losing their mother, but that they wouldn't be torn apart by what was sure to be a messy divorce?

With a sigh, he climbed into his silver Ford Super

Duty and pulled out of the drive. And as he passed Bill Krenek's place minutes later, Jake's mind automatically shifted to Alli.

His chest squeezed with a familiar ache. *God, forgive me for what I did to her. My actions were nothing more than pure selfishness.*

Not so unlike Bethany's.

The realization had him tightening his grip on the steering wheel as he all but gasped for air. No wonder Alli hated him.

When he arrived at Plowman's a short time later, he grabbed a small basket as he entered, then promptly filled it with the milk, bacon and bread before continuing past everything from cowboy hats to fertilizer spreaders, to live bait, until he neared the bakery. He was fond of their peach pie. Maybe they'd have one left.

He made a beeline for the wooden display rack, coming to an abrupt halt when a woman wearing a camo ball cap with a brunette ponytail hanging out the back stepped in front of him.

"Excuse me, ma—" Before he could finish, he was looking into those brilliant blue eyes he remembered so well. "Alli."

She looked as awkward as he felt. Dressed in jeans, a gray T-shirt and boots, she looked very much the way he remembered her. Only different. Better. Save for the trepidation in her eyes.

"You look like you've been riding," he finally said.

"Yeah." Her nod was exaggerated. "It was a nice distraction."

Distraction from what? Him? The awkwardness of yesterday?

Finally, she squared her shoulders. "How did the interviews go?"

"On paper, they'd seemed promising." He shrugged. "In reality, not so much."

She seemed to wince. "I'm sorry. But I don't blame you for having high standards. One can never be too cautious in today's world."

"You'd understand that probably better than anyone around here." With her having worked for CPS and him a police officer, they'd seen a lot of things he was sure they'd both rather forget.

Meeting his gaze, she said, "I'm sincerely praying you'll find the right person, Jake. I know it's not easy for you to entrust your children's care to someone else."

Could she be the right person?

He quickly shook off the notion. Not only would she never go for it, it was a bad idea all the way around. "I appreciate that."

She nodded. "I should go before this ice cream melts."

Only then did he notice the three pints of Blue Bell in the handheld basket. Pecan Pralines 'n Cream. The corners of his mouth lifted. That'd always been both their favorite. How many times had they had to do rock paper scissors to decide who got the last bite? And then they'd usually end up deciding to split it, no matter how small the amount.

She turned. "I'll, uh, see you around maybe."

"Yeah." He watched her go, his craving for pie gone.

God, I have no idea how to make things right between me and Alli, but I would do anything to earn her trust again.

Chapter Three

When a pint of Blue Bell couldn't cure Alli's uneasiness, she knew she was in trouble.

And considering she'd eaten *all three* pints since picking them up at Plowman's yesterday afternoon and was still wound up, she knew it was time to acknowledge that gentle nudging God had been giving her. The one that had begun to feel more like a cattle prod.

After supper with her dad and Francie, Alli hurried upstairs to her apartment to grab the papers she'd printed earlier, then gathered her keys and wallet and briefly gave herself a once-over in the mirror before heading out the door.

As she pulled her red Jeep Wrangler out of the drive and started up the two-lane road lined with bluebonnets and Indian paintbrush, she had every confidence she was doing the right thing. Though that didn't make it any easier. Her stomach felt as though she'd just stepped off one of those topsy-turvy roller coasters. And it had nothing to do with the ice cream.

No, this was all about Jake and the fact that she needed a job. Sure, the bond they'd once shared had been defaced by a single transgression that had changed everything she'd once believed about him, but that didn't mean she should allow his two beautiful children to suffer for his carelessness.

A few minutes later, she sucked in a breath as her Jeep bumped over the cattle guard into Jake's lengthy drive. The last time she'd been there, the place had belonged to his parents. According to her father, after Jake's dad, Ralph, passed away, Jake took over running the ranch and he and his family moved into his parents' house while Joanna bought a small place in Hope Crossing proper.

Now, as Alli rounded a curve, gravel grinding beneath her heavy-duty tires, the Cape Cod–style house with dormers and a wraparound porch perched on a gentle rise came into view, sparking memories of campfires, racing horses across the pasture and goofing off at the swimming hole that sat beyond the Walker house. Since neither she nor Jake had any siblings and she preferred playing in the dirt over dolls, they'd forged a bond at a young age. One she never imagined would be so easily broken.

If only her heart hadn't strayed to thoughts of something more than just friendship.

Shaking off the unwanted recollection, she continued up the winding drive, noting that the once pale yellow house was now a soothing shade of gray and the black shutters had been removed, allowing the white trim to lend a more casual look. Combined with the slate-colored metal roof that had replaced the time-worn shingles, it looked like a brand-new house. Sleek and modern, while remaining true to its surroundings.

Her gaze continued to roam the once-familiar spread, noting a new three-sided metal barn with a stretch of covered pens had replaced the dilapidated wooden one beyond the far end of the house. And as she drew closer, she spotted Jake just inside it with both kids nearby.

He looked up when a dog barked, no doubt announcing Alli's arrival. A moment later, Jake stepped outside, reminding her of old times, except she would've been on her horse or a bicycle back then.

She eased her Jeep to a stop beneath the picturesque live oak dripping with Spanish moss that gently swayed in the barely there breeze. With a deep breath, she shot up a prayer for courage, folded the papers she'd brought and tucked them into her back pocket before opening the door.

The moment her sneakers hit the gravel, two dogs greeted her, their tails wagging in silent glee. Alli couldn't help laughing. The short-haired brindle-colored one was as big as a small horse, while the fuzzy white one looked like a tiny stuffed animal.

"Well, hello there." She swung her door closed before showing each of them a little affection. "You two are quite the pair."

The sound of rapidly approaching footsteps had her looking up to see Maddy racing toward her, wearing a pink T-shirt, purple leggings and cowboy boots, her long curls flying, while her father moved at a more leisurely pace with Connor in his arms and curiosity written all over his face.

"Miss Alli! You're here!" Maddy flung her arms around Alli's hips and squeezed for all she was worth.

Alli reveled in the child's exuberance and gave her little shoulders a squeeze. "How are you?"

Maddy peered up at her with light blue eyes that could melt anyone's heart. "We're going to feed the calf. Wanna come?"

Shielding her own eyes from the sun that hovered

above the horizon, Alli watched as Jake neared, her heart thudding against her ribs. Had a dirty, brown T-shirt, dusty jeans and boots ever looked so good? Even better than when they were in high school.

Being a football player, Jake had always worked out, but age had lent a more natural look to his sculpting. One any woman could appreciate. Even if they had no interest in the man himself.

"Feed a calf?" She looked up at the man who was a good six inches taller than her five-five. "Mama gone or'd she reject it?"

"She's doing her best to reject him," he said. "I've got her in the pen with him, though, hoping she'll come around. But in the meantime—"

"You've got to keep him alive."

The corners of his mouth lifted. "You can take the girl out of the country, but you can't take the country out of the girl."

"Never."

The big dog nudged her hand.

Turning to pet both pups again—and give her something else to consider besides Jake—she said, "And who are these two?"

"The mastiff there is Beauty."

Alli gave the gentle giant a rub. "Nice to meet you, Beauty."

Meanwhile, Maddy awkwardly scooped the little dog into her arms. "And this is Beast."

A chuckle spilled out of Alli. "You don't look like much of a beast to me." She scratched his chin while his tail wagged.

Straightening, she slipped her hands into the pockets of her skinny jeans and visually explored the vibrant pastures dotted with healthy cattle. "The place looks great." She dared a glance at Jake. "You've done a nice job."

Maddy set Beast on the ground and took hold of Alli's hand. "C'mon, let's go feed the calf." The girl tugged with all of her might, leaving Alli little choice but to follow.

The familiar aromas of hay, earth and cattle reminded her of her childhood and helping her father. At her dad's place, she was the one who'd cared for their nurse cows, any orphans or sickly animals. As a result, she'd learned enough to know that she did *not* want to be a veterinarian after all.

"Aw." Her heart melted when she spotted the caramel-and-white calf, its sad eyes rimmed with pink. Poor little fella. His furry hide was a mess, a sure sign his mama had failed to tend to him.

Reaching through the metal rungs, she gave him a good rub, her gaze narrowing on his mama across the way. "That mean old mama of yours needs to come to her senses and take care of you."

Maddy came alongside her, holding a large plastic bottle of colostrum replacement the calf would need to survive and protect against disease.

"Oh, look at that." Alli smiled as the calf poked his nose through the rungs, trying to get to the bottle. "You know what's in there, don't you, buddy?"

By the time the calf latched on and Connor pushed his way between Alli and his sister, Alli sensed Jake behind her.

"What brings you by?" His voice held an air of caution.

She lifted a shoulder, her attention still fixed on the hungry calf. "Guilt."

"Over what?"

"Never allowing you to apologize."

"While I didn't necessarily like it, I s'pose it's understandable."

"For the first couple of years, maybe." Turning, she looked up at him. "Between then and now, well, that was not only immature, but rather selfish of me."

Arms crossed over his chest, making his biceps look even bigger, he stared at her. "The Alli I used to know was never selfish."

Unable to come up with a response, she shrugged, her focus on the bags of feed behind him instead of the man himself.

"He's all done, Daddy." Maddy held up the now empty bottle.

Jake took hold of it and moved to the utility sink along the wall to rinse it out.

"Can you play with us?" Maddy peered up at Alli, bouncing up and down, her brother mimicking her every move.

"It's about time for you two to get ready for bed," Jake called over his shoulder.

Without missing a beat, Maddy peered up at Alli and said, "Can you stay and read to us?"

Only then did Alli realize she should have called Jake first, perhaps tried to set up a meeting with him when the kids weren't around. Because even though she was willing to care for his children, that didn't automatically mean he'd be on board with the idea.

She definitely needed to speak with him in private.

Wiping his hands with a paper towel, he moved toward them. "Word on the street is that you're a spectacular storybook reader."

She felt her cheeks heat. "What can I say? I'm still a kid at heart."

"Pleeeeze." Maddy put her little hands together in a prayer pose.

"Peeeze," Connor mimicked his sister.

Jake shrugged. "If you can say no to that, then you're a stronger person than I am."

She looked from the kids to Jake and back again before releasing a sigh. "Nope, I'm too weak."

"Come on, then." He motioned for her and the kids to follow him. "Perhaps this'll play in my favor."

Alli fell in line behind him, smiling when little hands slipped into each of hers. "How so?"

"Well, no story until they're ready for bed. So the anticipation alone should make that process go a lot quicker."

"Ah. You are a wise man, Mr. Walker."

They strolled across the drive and onto the grass, continuing along the side of the house and around to the back where there was an attached carport. On the covered porch, Beauty lay in front of the door while Beast hopped up on all fours, his tail wagging.

Jake toed out of his boots, as did Maddy.

Meanwhile, Connor plopped down on his bottom and tried to follow suit. Just when he began to get frustrated, his father said, "Hold on, buddy. I gotcha."

As Jake opened the door to the laundry room moments later, an unexpected nervousness settled over Alli. This wasn't the house she'd once been free to enter without knocking. It no longer belonged to Joanna. This was the house Jake had shared with his wife, where they'd built a family, until tragedy tore them apart.

"You coming?"

She looked up to see Jake and the kids standing inside the cluttered space, staring at her.

Nodding, she toed out of her own shoes and followed him into the house that, surprisingly, still felt familiar despite the different decor. Toys were scattered about the living room that had the same distressed vinyl plank floor as the hallway and kitchen, something Jake seemed rather self-conscious about, apologizing for the mess.

The kids' rooms were on the opposite end of the house, separated by a bathroom. Maddy's cowgirl-themed room had once belonged to Jake, while Connor's sports-themed space had been Joanna's craft room. Alli had been in awe of all the fabric and yarn the woman always seemed to have for her quilting and knitting projects.

At Maddy's request, Alli helped her choose her pajamas, wash up, and brush her hair and teeth, while Jake assisted Connor. As the sky grew dark outside, they gathered in Connor's room, Maddy in her daddy's lap, Connor in Alli's while she read them *Goodnight Moon.* The children's classic had always been one of Alli's favorites.

Connor's eyes were closed by the time she finished, so Jake took hold of the boy and settled him under the covers while Alli walked Maddy to her room.

"I wish you could read to us every night," the girl said as she crawled under her brightly colored quilt Alli was certain Joanna had made.

"You'd get used to it then and it wouldn't be special anymore."

"But you make them more funner."

"Okay, princess." Jake swept into the room, bringing with him the aroma of fresh air, hard work and bubble-gum-scented hand soap. He leaned over his daughter's bed, settling a hand on either side of her, and kissed her forehead. "Did you thank Miss Alli for reading to you?"

She peered around her father's arm. "Thank you, Miss Alli."

"You're welcome." With that, she returned to the living room, allowing Jake a moment alone with his daughter. Not to mention to psych herself up for what she was about to propose.

Looking at the baby photos on the wall, she could absolutely see herself caring for Jake's children, preparing meals and even helping keep the house tidy. There was no denying Jake was overwhelmed. And it would be a nice way for her to spend the next several months.

"That might be the easiest time I've ever had getting them to bed." Jake rounded the corner and paused in front of the brown leather sofa. "Thank you. I'm sure you weren't planning on all of that when you came over."

"No, but it's okay. I enjoy reading to little ones."

"Uh, what I witnessed in there wasn't just reading, Alli—you make the story jump right off the page. I always thought *Goodnight Moon* was kind of boring, but you made it fun."

"I learned from the best."

"Your mama?"

"Yep. She used to make up stories for me and use all sorts of goofy voices. I'm not imaginative enough to create my own stories, but I find that if I add a little silliness and unexpected twists to something they've heard countless times, the kids stay engaged."

"That's quite a gift."

"Thank you. I enjoy it as much as the kids." Reaching for the papers in her back pocket, she said, "So, my apology earlier wasn't the only reason I came over here."

"Oh?" Jake's gaze narrowed. He crossed his arms over his chest, as though he was preparing for battle.

Unfolding the papers, she attempted to smooth the creases before passing them to him. "I'd like to be considered for the nanny position."

The mixture of surprise and skepticism in his eyes when he took hold of the documents had her feeling suddenly nervous.

"I've been with Child Protective Services for the past eight years and am currently working toward a career in teaching."

He looked from the papers to her. "Meaning you'll be leaving at some point in the near future."

She nodded. "I expect I'll be here until late fall, perhaps the end of the year." She rocked back on her heels. "I've included a list of references."

"I don't need any references." He refolded the papers. "I know everything I need to know about you, Alli." He handed them back to her, his eyes darkening to a steely gray. "However, my kids need stability. And while there are no guarantees with anyone I eventually hire, I can't, in good conscience, hire you when I know you won't be sticking around. So I'm sorry, but the answer is no."

"You did *what*?" Standing just outside the barn, clad in denim capris and a brown T-shirt, his mother glared at him the next morning while the kids fed the calf. "Jake, have you lost your marbles?" She cut a glance toward his children before shooting daggers at him once again. "Alli—" she whispered the name "—would make a perfect nanny and you know it."

"Not if she's going to be leaving soon."

His mother shook her head, her lips pursed. "Didn't we discuss some other less-than-perfect scenarios? Why would it be any different with Alli? You can still keep looking for someone to fill the position permanently. And when you do, you'll have a seamless transition."

"But what about the kids? I don't want them to get too attached to her."

"Finished, Daddy." Maddy approached with the empty bottle and handed it to him before wiping her hands on her purple shirt. "Can I go play on the swing set?"

His gaze drifted to the front yard of the house and the pint-size playset beneath the oak tree. "Yes, you may."

"I go, too?" Connor squinted up at him, looking like a miniature Jake in his jeans and John Deere T-shirt.

"Sure, buddy."

"Mimi will be there in a minute," his mother called after them as they took off with the dogs. Returning her attention to Jake, she perched her fists on her hips. "I don't think it's the kids you're worried about growing attached to Alli. I think you're worried *you'll* get attached to her."

He started toward the barn to rinse out the bottle. "Mom, I'm a grown man."

Undeterred, she stepped in front of him. "Who was once very fond of Alli Krenek."

They stared at each other, neither wanting to be the first to look away.

"Mimi!" Connor called.

She broke eye contact first, taking hold of Jake's arm. "Coming, Connor." She gave a squeeze, her gaze bouncing briefly to Jake's. "This is your call, son. Just remember, it's about them—" she poked her other thumb toward the kids "—not you."

He moved to the sink as she walked away, the knot that had been in his gut since sending Alli away last night tightening. Was that what he was doing? Making decisions based on his feelings instead of what was best for Maddy and Connor?

He turned on the water. Then again, just look how they'd latched on to Alli already. How would they react when she became a fixture in their lives and then was suddenly gone?

They survived losing their mother.

They were younger then.

It's not like she's going to be with them 24/7.

He rinsed out the bottle and set it aside to dry before turning off the water. Eyeing the calf and cow, he noticed she was finally letting the little fella near her. Jake had even seen her sniffing him—better than kicking at him the way she had been.

An image of Alli here in the barn last night played across his mind. She'd been pushing Jake away for seventeen years. And yet when she'd offered him the one thing he'd thought he wanted, even prayed for, he'd done the exact same thing he'd done seventeen years ago. Shot himself in the foot. Because once again, he'd made it all about him.

He removed his worn straw Resistol long enough to drag a hand through his hair.

Walker, you have got to be the biggest numbskull on the face of this planet.

With a groan, he turned, digging in his pocket for his keys as he strode toward his truck. "Mom?"

She looked his way, shielding her eyes from the sun.

"I'll be back in a bit."

After she waved him off, he jumped into his truck, fired up the engine and sent gravel flying as he started down the drive.

God, yesterday You presented me with the very thing I had asked for and yet I dismissed it. Obviously I'm just as thickheaded as I was seventeen years ago. So, Lord, for Maddy and Connor's sake, I'm begging You for one more opportunity. Please let Alli agree to care for my kids.

Seeing her Jeep in Bill's driveway, Jake parked behind it and hurried up the steps, taking them two at a time. He knocked on the door. "Alli, please. I need to talk to you." He continued knocking, but there was no answer.

Was she inside and ignoring him, or was she someplace else?

He hurried down to the main house and knocked on the door.

"Jake?" Francie smiled up at him, wiping her hands on a dish towel. "What brings you by?"

"Is Alli here?"

"No, she took one of the horses out for a ride about an hour ago. Said she needed to clear her head."

"If you see her before I do, could you please tell her that I need to talk to— Wait. On second thought, don't tell her anything. But if you'd please text or call me when she gets back, I'd be much obliged."

Her dark eyes watched him curiously. Finally, her smile returned, and she nodded. "I can do that."

Returning to his truck, he pondered his next move. When he recalled seeing her at Plowman's the other day, he knew just what to do.

Twenty minutes later, he returned to Bill's, armed with two pints of Pecan Pralines 'n Cream tucked inside a small, soft-sided cooler he kept in the truck. A little peace offering couldn't hurt, could it?

Again, he parked behind the red Jeep. And at the same time his phone buzzed with a text, Alli emerged from the house, pulling the door closed behind her before starting toward the stairs.

Taking hold of the cooler, he couldn't seem to get out of his truck fast enough. "Alli!"

Sunglasses covered her eyes as she jerked her head in his direction. Her jeans were dusty, the sleeves of her T-shirt rolled up, her hair in a ponytail. And he couldn't help noticing the way she defiantly squared her shoulders.

"I have something for you." He tossed the door closed as he started toward her. Unzipping the six-pack-sized cooler, he pulled out the plastic bag and offered it to her.

Moving her sunglasses to the top of her head, she looked from the bag to him. "What's this?"

He hesitated. "A peace offering."

Taking hold, she peered inside, one brow lifting as her gaze shifted to his. "Are these *both* for me? Or are you hoping I'll share?"

"They're yours. That is, unless you *want* to share." He was going about this all wrong. He blew out a long breath and looked at her. "I was wrong."

Her lips pursed, she nodded. "Not the first time."

"I don't know what I was thinking last night. I must've been brain dead or something because you are exactly the kind of nanny I want Maddy and Connor to have. Someone who genuinely cares for them and will put their interests first. Yeah, it stinks that you won't be able to stay long term, especially when I doubt we'll be able to find anyone who could hold a candle to you. But if I promise to stop behaving like a jerky seventeen-year-old and keep the freezer stocked with your—*our*—favorite ice cream, would you *please* agree to care for my children?"

She watched him intently, her expression giving away nothing.

He could feel the sweat beading on his forehead, and it wasn't even that hot outside.

Finally, the corners of her mouth lifted. "I wondered how long it would take you to change your mind."

"What do you mean?"

"Seventeen years may have passed since the last time we were together for any length of time, but I can still read you like a book, Walker."

"Are you telling me you knew I was going to change my mind?"

She lifted a shoulder. "Suspected."

"Man." He rubbed the back of his neck. "I'm gonna have to work on that. I can't have you knowing what I'm thinking even before I do."

"Why not? Isn't that how we've always been?"

He puffed out a chuckle. "I guess so." Sobering, he looked at her again. "Does this mean you'll accept the position?"

She tilted her head. "On one condition."

"Anything."

"Always be truthful with me."

"I'll do my best."

"That's not what I asked for, Jake. I don't want you to simply try, I want you to do it."

He looked everywhere but at her. What she was asking wasn't difficult. But he did have a habit of skirting the truth, especially if he knew said truth might hurt someone. Then again, it did always seem to back to bite him. So perhaps a change was in order.

"In that case, I promise I'll always be truthful with you. Even if it kills me."

Chapter Four

What had she gotten herself into?

Alli had arrived at Jake's right at seven the next morning, after agreeing she would shadow Joanna for a couple days so she could familiarize herself with the kids' routines, their likes and dislikes, the house, and, of course, her duties. But even before the kids had finished their breakfast, Alli discovered one thing was sorely lacking at Jake's house.

Structure.

Joanna fed the kids when they were hungry—and they were always hungry—then fretted when they didn't eat the lunch she'd prepared. She had their favorite shows memorized and played them all day long. Even when the kids should've been napping. Instead, she simply sat with them on the sofa, hoping they'd fall asleep. Which they didn't.

No doubt about it, Joanna was a wonderful grandmother who loved doting on Maddy and Connor. Yet while Alli couldn't fault the woman for spoiling her grandchildren, she wanted so much more for those kiddos. She wanted to see them thrive. To be engaged.

Learning while still having fun, like when she'd taken them outside to play on their little playset this morning.

Alli had pointed out a couple of wrens busily building a nest, along with some tiny toads and a spotted whip-tailed lizard. Though Beast had quickly decided the lizard was a toy for him and chased it across the yard.

Then there was the house. Upon first glance, it appeared tidy enough. But behind the scenes, chaos reigned. Joanna had spent half the morning digging through drawers and piles of laundry, both clean and dirty, looking for Maddy's favorite pony shirt. Generous counter space in the kitchen was so cluttered there was barely any room for food prep. Even the island was littered with papers.

Now as Alli stared into the walk-in pantry that one would find difficult to actually walk into because of all the odds and ends strewn across the floor, not to mention the jam-packed shelves overflowing with canned goods, half-empty boxes and bags, countertop appliances, empty storage containers, and other random items, her heart went out to both Jake and Joanna. The two of them had been thrust into roles neither particularly wanted—single father and full-time caregiver—and were simply doing their best to get by.

She felt sorry for them. Their lives had been thrown into chaos when Jake's wife died. Yet neither wanted the children to suffer. So they kept putting one foot in front of the other, doing whatever was needed to keep things as normal as possible and making sure the kids knew they were loved. After all, structure is the least of one's worries when simply trying to survive.

In that moment, Alli couldn't help wondering if that nudging God had been giving her wasn't more of a calling. Jake and Joanna were overwhelmed. And the state of Jake's house had a lot to do with that. Bringing order to the place would certainly lift some of his burden and allow him to enjoy his children even more.

"Connor's out." Joanna moved past Alli to retrieve a plastic pitcher of iced tea from the side-by-side refrigerator beside the pantry.

Glancing into the living room on the opposite side of the hallway that separated it from the kitchen, Alli spotted the boy curled up on the couch with a blanket, eyes closed and those two fingers in his mouth.

"It's after four, though." She looked at Joanna. "I thought their bedtime was eight."

"On a perfect day, yes." Jake's mother added more tea to the ice that remained in her mason jar. "But when the kids nap late in the day like this, it's a struggle for Jake to meet that goal."

Yet another reason for Alli to get these kids on a schedule. When they knew what was expected of them, things generally ran more smoothly.

"Has it always been this way?"

Joanna returned the pitcher to the fridge, shaking her head. "Bethany always put them in their beds to nap right after lunch. Of course, the kids were younger then." Jake's mother released a sigh. "I suppose I'm a soft touch, though. I just can't stand to hear them cry."

Alli couldn't help smiling at the woman, who suddenly looked rather defeated. She reached for her hand. "That's because you're their grandmother. And a pretty spectacular one at that."

Joanna pulled her in for a hug. "I'm so glad you're here, Alli." Releasing her, she added, "I'm certain my grandchildren feel the same way."

"I hope so." She again glanced into the disorganized mess that was the pantry. "Do you have something planned for supper?"

Another sigh. "I set some ground beef out to thaw, but I haven't decided what to do with it yet."

Alli studied Jake's mother, noting the dark circles under her eyes. Joanna wasn't old by any means, but in her early sixties, she wasn't a spring chicken either. She should be enjoying life, not raising children. Not that she would ever complain.

"In that case, would you like me to prepare something?"

Joanna's face brightened. "That would be wonderful, dear. You're sure you don't mind?"

"Not at all. I'll be doing it from here on out anyway."

Joanna's smile erased the harsh lines that had marred her beautiful features only moments ago. "In that case, by my guest." She grabbed her glass and returned to the living room where Maddy sat cross-legged on the floor, Beauty at her side, gawking at the flat screen perched atop a console, looking as though she could fall asleep any minute, too.

After discovering a half-empty bag of Tater Tots and some mixed vegetables in the deepest recesses of the freezer, some cheese in the fridge and a can of cream of mushroom soup in the pantry, Alli settled on a Tater Tot casserole. It was quick, easy and bubbling in the oven when Jake entered the house at five thirty.

"Something smells delicious."

Alli looked up from the dishwasher she was unloading as a hatless Jake appeared in the hallway.

"Daddy!" Maddy sprang to her feet and rushed to meet him.

Just like in the nursery, he readily lifted her into his

arms, his smile wide. At least until he spotted a still-sleeping Connor.

Getting him to bed tonight was going to be a chore. One Jake wasn't looking forward to, if his expression was any indication.

"Alli cooked." Joanna strolled into the kitchen.

Glass in hand, Alli opened one cupboard after the next, trying to determine what went where.

"Glasses go over here, dear." Joanna opened the cupboard to the left of the sink—the one that was closest to the table yet farthest from the refrigerator. Meanwhile, plates and bowls were in the cupboard beside the refrigerator, as far from the table as they could possibly get.

The timer went off.

Alli set the clean mason jar in the cupboard, grabbed two pot holders and retrieved the casserole from the oven as a cry echoed from the living room.

Jake promptly set Maddy on the floor and went to his son, who didn't appear very happy about having his sleep interrupted by all the noise.

Meanwhile, Joanna grabbed a crumpled bag of fish crackers from the pantry and hurried toward them. "He's probably ready for a snack." She offered the bag to the boy, but Connor simply buried his face in his daddy's neck.

Just as well, since supper was ready.

While the casserole rested atop the stove, Alli finished unloading the dishwasher and set the table.

Mission accomplished, she joined everyone in the living room. "I'm going to head out now, but supper is ready, so y'all are free to eat whenever." She stooped beside Maddy. "Can I have hugs?"

"But I don't want you to go." The girl's bottom lip pooched out, tugging at Alli's heart.

"I'll be back tomorrow."

Maddy's eyes brightened. "You will?"

"Yes. And maybe we can do some more exploring outside."

"Yay!" She threw her little arms around Alli's neck.

A moment later, Alli stood, eyeing Connor, who was still in his father's arms. She smoothed a hand over his back. "I'll see you tomorrow, okay, buddy?"

Still struggling to wake up, he sent her a hint of a smile as he rested his cheek against his daddy's shoulder, fingers in his mouth.

With that, she waved to the two adults and made her way down the hall, through the laundry room that had more piles than she could count, and outside. Stepping off the porch, she drew in a breath of fresh air as the door opened behind her.

"Wait up, Alli." Jake's long strides had him beside her in no time. Falling in line with her, he said, "Is everything okay? I thought you might like to stay and have supper with us."

"Thanks, but Dad and Francie are expecting me. Besides, I have an online test I need to take tonight."

"Ah." Hands tucked in his pockets, his steps slowed as they reached her Jeep near the oak tree. "You're sure you're okay, though? You seem a little, I don't know, distant."

Probably because she was mentally reorganizing his house and formulating ideas to engage his children.

Pausing beside the bumper, she smiled. "I'm fine. Really. I'm just trying to make sure I have a handle on everything so Joanna can start enjoying her freedom next week." And Alli could begin bringing some order to Jake's house which would, in return, make his life easier. "I do have a question, though."

"Sure." Those gray eyes of his were fixed on her, as though he couldn't wait to hear what she had to say.

Dismissing the sudden flutter in her heart, she looked away. "Would you mind if I did a little reorganizing in the kitchen and laundry room?" For starters, anyway.

He chuckled, rubbing the back of his neck. "Yeah, that pantry has gotten *way* out of hand, along with just about everything else around here. I get the feeling my mother is overwhelmed. Just another reason why it was so important I hire some help."

Alli was pretty sure Joanna wasn't the only one who was overwhelmed. And she found herself longing to lift his burden.

"So yes," he continued. "You're free to do whatever you like."

"Great. I'll see you tomorrow, then." Turning, she opened the door and climbed inside, invigorated by the challenge that lay ahead. Caring for Maddy and Connor was a pleasure in and of itself, but realizing she'd been presented with the opportunity to make all of their lives better gave her a new resolve. And she could hardly wait to get started.

Jake headed toward the house late Friday afternoon with a spring in his step. His mother's traveling companion had called her earlier in the day, asking if she'd like to meet for dinner and do some shopping, so his mother was already gone and only Alli remained at the house with the kids. Something that excited him more than it probably should. But he had such a yearning to reconnect with the woman who had once been his closest friend. He'd always felt like a better person when Alli was around. At least until he wasn't.

Stepping onto the back porch, he nudged the regret

away. Perhaps he could convince Alli to stay for supper instead of rushing off again. Last night, he found himself overthinking her quick departure. Did she not want to be anywhere near him? Had she been overwhelmed by the kids? Or his mother? Maybe it was the house. She'd mentioned she wanted to do some reorganizing.

He toed off his boots and set them on the boot dryer before continuing into the laundry room. As he dropped his hat on its hook and squeezed past the overgrown pile of clothes and towels opposite the washer, he was reminded that he needed to do a load before Sunday so the kids would have something to wear to church.

Rounding the corner into the hallway, he was greeted with the familiar, not to mention oh so appealing, aroma of bacon and something else he couldn't put his finger on. But whatever it was had his stomach growling.

Approaching the kitchen/living area, he couldn't help noticing that things were kind of quiet. No silly songs or goofy voices. Then he realized the television wasn't on.

"Wook, Miss Awee," he heard Connor say. "I make a wion. Whowah."

Jake chuckled at his son's lion roar.

"Very good, Connor."

Following the voices, Jake moved into the kitchen where Alli sat at the table with the kids. It appeared they were painting.

"Daddy, wook." Connor's smile was wide as he held up an orange-streaked paper plate with one hand while swiping a paint-covered finger on the other hand across his shirt.

Panic momentarily set in, until Jake realized he was wearing a bib. "That's awesome, buddy." He moved beside the newspaper-covered table to see Maddy creating her own paper plate masterpiece with shades of pink and purple. "Whatcha working on there, Madikins?"

Focusing on her work, she said, "A pony."

Of course it was. His daughter was obsessed with horses. Ponies, in particular.

Alli looked up at him. "I found the paints in the pantry. Along with the paper plates." Pointing to the island, she continued. "I did a little sorting while the kids napped."

"Napped? How did you manage that?"

"I read to them."

That meant he had a shot at getting them to bed on time tonight.

Standing, she started toward the island. "I found a few items in the pantry that were expired." She settled a hand atop the small pile on the counter. "I thought I'd let you go through them so you could see what you were interested in replacing."

Joining her, he eyed the items. "Probably impulse purchases." Something either sounded good, or the kids had talked him into it.

Noting an oblong pan on the stove, he went to investigate. "Is this peach cobbler?"

"It is. There were some frozen sliced peaches that were on the verge of freezer burn, so I thought I'd find a way to use them instead of throwing them away."

"So the fact that peach cobbler has always been one of my favorites didn't play into your decision?"

She shook her head. "Not really."

"How 'bout the fact that it's one of *your* favorites? Or used to be, anyway."

"Well, if you'll notice, there is a little bit missing from one corner."

"Couldn't wait, could you?"

"I prefer to think of it as quality control."

"And?"

She sent him a thumbs-up before returning to the table. "There's bacon-wrapped meatloaf, mashed potatoes and some green beans keeping warm in the oven."

"That's why I'm smelling bacon. It all sounds delicious."

"I'm hungry," said Maddy.

"I, too," said Connor.

"Let's get things cleaned up, then." Alli put lids on the paints and set their artwork atop the island to dry.

Only then did he notice that all of the papers that had covered the space this morning were now in a single neat stack.

"Jake, would you help them wash their hands, please?"

"Sure thing." He scooted a stool in front of the stainless-steel sink for Maddy while he wrapped one arm around Connor and held him over the basin.

By the time he'd finished, the paint supplies were not only put away, but the table had been set.

He dried the kids' hands and set his son on the floor, his gaze moving to Alli at the refrigerator as she filled Connor's sippy cup with milk. "Would you care to join us for supper? Enjoy the fruits of your labor."

"Sorry, but the folks and I are headed over to the Knights of Columbus Hall for their Friday night fish fry." She returned the gallon jug to the fridge and closed the door. "Besides, I have a curriculum to plan for next week." She secured the lid.

"Curriculum? For what?"

Returning to the table, she set the cup next to Connor's plastic plate. "I'd like to engage the kids a bit more with some hands-on learning. Less watching other people or characters experience things and, instead, experiencing new things themselves."

"Like you were doing just now, or are we talking field trips?"

She shrugged. "We may make the occasional trip to the library, but we live in the country. There's a lot to explore right around here."

He couldn't help smiling. "Like we did when we were kids."

"Exactly." She started to turn away then stopped. "Does your mom still have that garden out back?"

"Yes, but it's been overgrown with weeds. She's got a raised bed at her place now."

"Would you mind if I clean it up? I think the kids would get a kick out of watching things grow, especially when they eat it."

He wasn't sure how helpful the kids would be, but they'd love playing in the dirt. "I like that idea. We're already in the prime of planting season, though, so you'll need to jump on it right away. I suppose I could weed and till the bed this weekend and have it ready to go for you Monday morning."

Her smile made his grow even bigger. "You can't till without someone watching the kids. Besides, I don't expect you to do the weeding when it was my idea. You've got enough on your plate already."

"What do you propose we do, then?"

"I have plans tomorrow morning, probably into early afternoon, but I could come by around three thirty, and we could all work on it together."

Together. He dared not read too much into that single word. It was an opening, though. One he had to explore.

"We might work up an appetite. If I were to throw something on the grill, would you join us for supper?"

She whisked past him to fill a glass with ice. "Why are you so determined to have me share a meal with you?"

He could say he wanted to show off his grilling prowess. Or that he missed having another adult to talk to. But he'd promised Alli he'd be truthful.

Watching as she pulled the pitcher of tea from the fridge, he said, "Because I miss having you as my friend. And while I know we can never recapture the friendship we once had, I'd like the opportunity to get to know the woman you've become."

Though her focus was on filling the glass, pink bloomed on her cheeks. "Way to go, Walker." She returned the container to the refrigerator and closed the door.

"What?"

She looked up at him. "You made it impossible for me to say no."

How could he not smile? "Hmm, perhaps you were on to something when you insisted I be honest."

She shook her head.

"So now it's your turn."

Her panicked gaze again lifted to his.

"Which would you prefer, steak or chicken?"

Her laugh was a nervous one. "Oh, I haven't changed that much."

He nodded. "In that case, steak it is."

Chapter Five

Alli could not have handpicked better weather for clearing the garden at Jake's on Saturday. Temperatures were in the seventies, the humidity was low and the sky was a beautiful azure.

While Jake maneuvered the tiller over the now weed-free garden, she dusted the dirt from her maroon Aggies T-shirt and adjusted her ball cap, watching Connor propel his ride-on toy tractor across the grass with Beauty at his side. A short distance away, Maddy tossed a ball, then giggled when Beast took off after it. Alli couldn't wait to teach the kids where food came from and about nature, the way her mother had taught her.

Angie Krenek had grown up poor and was a firm believer of making the most of what the good Lord provided. She loved working in her garden and had instilled that same appreciation in Alli. Sadly, Alli's apartment in the city hadn't been conducive to gardening, so the best she'd been able to manage in recent years were a few tomato and pepper plants grown in pots on her balcony.

Here in the country, though, there was plenty of space. And Francie, an avid gardener in her own right, had offered several varieties of seedlings, including tomatoes, cucumbers, squash and beans. Though any planting would have to wait until Monday. Just one of the many things Alli had planned for next week.

Her trip to Brenham this morning had her coming away with a plethora of craft supplies and age-appropriate activity books, along with an elementary writing tablet so she could help Maddy with her letters. And a stop at the dollar store had yielded several inexpensive plastic baskets in a variety of sizes that would help bring some much-needed order to Jake's pantry.

No doubt about it, Alli was going to be one busy beaver next week. But first she had to make it through today.

She could kick herself for agreeing to stay for supper. But like those days of old, Jake had said just the right thing to win her over. Now angst had her stomach tied in such a knot that she probably wouldn't be able to eat. Working alongside her childhood friend was one thing. But sitting down to eat with him was too…intimate. Even with two children in the mix.

Dining together meant conversing. Engaging beyond the superficial. And where Jake Walker was involved, that could be a risky endeavor. Even after all these years, they knew each other too well. Shared too many memories. Their lives had been entwined for so long, she'd be hard-pressed to think of anything that didn't include him.

They say old habits die hard. But allowing Jake access to her heart was one habit Alli couldn't afford to revisit.

The tiller fell silent and Alli turned as Jake started her way. Even sweaty and dirty, the man was far too appealing.

Shifting her focus to the rich soil he'd incorporated

some peat and compost into, she breathed in the earthy aroma. "That looks so much better than all those weeds." She dared a glance at him. "And soon it'll be filled with heathy plants the kids can watch grow and harvest."

He eyed her intently, the corners of his mouth tilting upward. "I get the feeling the kids aren't the only ones excited about this little project." He tugged off his work gloves. "But then, I imagine gardening holds some fond memories for you, doesn't it?" He'd know that better than anyone.

Nodding, she said, "I still remember the first time Mama let me plant a small section in her garden. Pickles were my favorite, so I chose pickling cucumbers, firmly believing I was growing pickles."

A low chuckle rumbled from him as he dragged an arm across his sweaty brow.

"Imagine my surprise when I bit into one and all I tasted was cucumber. I thought I'd done something wrong."

He eyed his children, his smile wide. "And if I recall correctly, that's when Angie gave you your first lesson in pickling."

Remembering her mother's patient tutelage made her smile. "Having to wait a month or more before I could enjoy the fruits of my labor was pure torture." The recollection of canning sparked another memory. "Speaking of fruit, do y'all still have your mulberry trees?" As kids she and Jake used to pick the berries and her mom would make jam.

"I believe so." He rubbed the shadow of a beard on his chin. "But it's been so long since anyone's paid attention to them I can't be certain. I think your mom was the only person who ever really appreciated them."

"Mama always said she couldn't let good fruit go to

waste because you never knew when you might find yourself wanting."

He looked down at her, his expression sober. "You miss her, don't you?"

Alli nodded. "Every day."

"I feel the same way about my dad." With a deep breath, Jake removed his ball cap long enough to run a hand through his hair while he took a sudden interest in the pasture. It was then Alli realized that he under-stood just how she felt. He and his father had always been close. Just like her and her mother.

Clearing his throat, he said, "I'll make a point to check on those trees."

"That's all right. The kids and I can walk over there one day. That way they can watch the berries as they progress from green to white to red and purple."

"Daddy, I'm hungry." They both turned as Maddy approached.

"Me, too." Jake glanced at his watch. "No wonder. It's almost six o'clock. I'd better get the grill going." He crossed the grass toward the carport and the gas grill sitting in the drive on the other side.

"What can I help with?" Alli hollered after him. "Po-tatoes? Salad?"

"I invited you," he hollered over his shoulder. "You shouldn't have to do a thing."

Connor abandoned his tractor to follow his daddy, so Alli trailed behind him with Maddy, trying to come up with something to keep her busy. Anything except sitting around, talking with Jake while he waited on her.

As Connor approached the carport, the toe of his sneaker hit the edge of the concrete, causing him to stumble.

Alli gasped and lurched forward, but she was too late.

Connor face-planted on the hard surface.

His cry was instantaneous.

Before she could get to the boy, Jake twisted and scooped him up in one fluid motion. Sorrow lined his face as he held his son close, swaying back and forth. "Shh. It's okay. Daddy's gotcha, buddy."

Maddy bounded onto the porch. "Connor, you gots to be careful."

Any other time, the comment would've made Alli chuckle. Maddy was definitely a big sister.

Moving beside Jake, Alli smoothed a hand over Connor's hair, wishing she'd thought to hold his hand. If she had, he wouldn't be hurting now. The little boy's face was red as he gasped for air and released another ear-piercing scream. A tiny amount of blood seeped from his split bottom lip, and a slight abrasion on his forehead had her fearing he might end up with a knot.

"I'll get some ice." While Jake continued to comfort his son, Alli hurried inside the house, feeling as though her heart might beat right out of her chest. If only she'd kept up with the boy.

She hastily grabbed a zip-top bag, filled it with as much ice as she could and still close it, then wrapped it in a towel. She was about to dash back outside when she remembered Maddy saying she was hungry, so she grabbed two small pouches of fruit snacks from the pantry before continuing outside.

Emerging onto the porch, Alli stopped in her tracks.

Jake sat in one of two camp chairs under the carport, cradling his son whose crying had faded to the occasional hiccup, his voice tender as he spoke soothing words, reminding Alli of the boy who'd been her best friend.

Jake had been twelve when his daddy bought him a

new horse. A beautiful buckskin. He'd been so proud of Mazie, and knowing how much Alli loved horses—or simply because she kept pestering him—he'd allowed her eleven-year-old self to ride the beautiful creature. But the filly that was still getting used to Jake was skittish and started bucking. Despite Jake's efforts to calm the horse, it ultimately sent Alli flying through the air. She'd landed like a rag doll and watched in horror as the horse reared up on its hind legs. She'd curled into a ball, trying desperately to protect herself. Thankfully, the horse only grazed the side of her head. But Jake was beside her in an instant, talking to her in the same tender manner he spoke to Connor now.

Jake was as kind as they came and had always watched out for Alli's best interests. Until she allowed one foolish, teenage mistake to rob her of the greatest friendship she'd ever had. All because she'd been too prideful to give him a second chance.

He still wanted to be her friend. But could she let go of the pain and embarrassment once and for all and forge a new bond? Her head told her to give it shot, while warning bells echoed in her heart.

God, I've forgiven Jake. But forgetting is a different story. How do I move forward when I can't seem to let go of the past?

Would he ever be able to regain Alli's trust?

It was a question Jake had been asking himself since Saturday. He'd even talked with his mother about it when he and the kids joined her for lunch at her place after church yesterday. Though her response only frustrated him more.

Give her time. Trust is something that has to be earned. And the one he hated the most: *You're just going to have to prove yourself.* How was he supposed to do that when Alli kept shutting him out?

He'd hoped working alongside her Saturday would feel like old times. But every time she appeared to be growing more comfortable, it was as though she'd catch herself and the wall she'd erected years ago went right back up.

And why was she beating herself up over Connor's fall? Despite Jake's reassurance that she wasn't responsible, she seemed determined to bear the blame.

Thankfully, she appeared more relaxed this morning. At his request, she'd arrived earlier than usual, bubbly and seemingly full of anticipation. He was slated to help Justin work cattle over at Prescott Farms, so he had to get an early start. Something that hadn't seemed to bother Alli in the least. Instead, she claimed she had plenty to keep her busy today.

Now, as he pulled up to the house shortly before six that evening, he could only pray this had, indeed, been a good day for her. And that, perhaps, he could convince her to stay for supper. Because somehow, someway, he would prove himself worthy in Alli's eyes. Bit by bit, little by little.

He climbed out of his truck into the humid air, eager to hear how Alli's first day alone with the kids had gone. It was rare that he didn't get an opportunity to stop by the house and at least check in. He'd intended to do that after trailering his horse back from Prescott Farms. But on his way, he'd noticed a couple strands of wire were missing from a section of fence. So after unloading Curly, he quickly unhitched the trailer and went straight back to mend the fence.

Then he had to change the oil in the tractor and throw out some fresh salt blocks for the cattle. If it hadn't been for needing to pick up a length of pipe at Plowman's to repair a broken one at one of the stock tanks, he wouldn't have even had time for lunch. He supposed his plans to move that cow and her calf to the pasture would have to wait until tomorrow. That's what he got for goofing around too much this weekend. He had phoned Alli, though, who assured him she had everything under control at the house.

He stepped onto the porch now, his gaze drifting to the garden. Alli had brought several seedlings with her this morning. And from the looks of things, they were now tucked neatly into the ground in perfect little rows. After setting his boots on the boot dryer, he continued into the laundry room where the smell of fabric softener and dryer sheets filled the air.

Closing the door, he dropped his hat on its hook, turned and froze. Eyes wide, he scanned the long, narrow space that was home to a top loading washer, a dryer and an upright freezer, all situated against the wall to his left, along with a short section of counter space intended for folding. Except—where were the piles of laundry he'd been too lazy to tackle over the weekend? The baskets of towels and sheets he'd procrastinated on for longer than he cared to admit? The plastic grocery sacks overflowing the one he kept shoving them into until they spilled onto the floor? And when was the last time he'd actually seen the countertop? It was usually covered with coats, jackets and whatever else needed a place to land.

Now the space was not only void of all that extraneous stuff, it was downright spotless. From the cupboards over the washer and dryer to the appliances and floor, the layer of dryer lint that once coated everything had been wiped away, allowing everything to shine.

How had Alli managed all of that in one day? With two children, no less.

Until now, the mess had never really bothered him much, unless he couldn't find something and had to dig. But seeing how it looked now had him feeling rather embarrassed. Alli must think him a complete slob.

"*M*! For *Maddy*!" His daughter's exuberant words drifted from the main part of the house.

"That's right," said Alli. "Very good."

Jake continued into the hallway, noting two large laundry baskets filled with neatly folded towels sitting just outside his bedroom door. The tangy aroma of something with tomato and garlic beckoned him in the opposite direction, though. Reaching that small section of hallway that separated the kitchen and living areas, he saw Alli sitting at the kitchen table with his children. She was holding what looked like a flash card in front of Connor.

"*C* is for *Connor*," she said with a smile.

"Yay, Connor!" Maddy cheered.

While the boy looked somewhat perplexed, he smiled and clapped right along with his sister as though he understood. For Alli's sake as well as Connor's, Jake was glad that the bump on the boy's head hadn't bruised or left a knot. Even his lip was fine by the time he went to bed last night. And that gave Jake a sense of relief. He hated to see his kiddos hurting.

Alli looked up then, her gaze colliding with his. And her smile did strange things to Jake's heart. "Look who's here, guys."

The children turned in unison. "Daddy!"

Maddy hopped out of her chair while Connor slid out of his, slowly easing his feet to the floor.

Jake awkwardly bent to hug each of them as they latched on to his legs. "How was your day?"

"It was T-riffic!" said Maddy. "We gots to help Miss Alli plant our garden and clean *and* make dinner. And she teached us how to draw our letters." Releasing him, his daughter scurried to the table, grabbed a sheet of paper then handed it to him when she returned.

Jake glanced at the page. "This looks like those worksheets we used to do back when we were learning our letters." Maddy's paper had examples of the letter *M*, followed by his daughter's attempts to mimic them. "You did great, Madikins."

She perched a hand on her hip, striking a sassy pose. "Connor just scribbled on his, but Miss Alli said that was okay since he's only two." His daughter definitely had a bit of a competitive streak.

"I'm sure your brother did the best he could." He glanced at Alli as she approached, noting the now-clutter-free countertops. "It appears you've had a busy day." He glanced from the spotless kitchen into the living room, where the toys that normally littered the space had all been returned to the bins tucked in one corner and there were even vacuum lines on the carpet. Throw in the laundry room and— "How did you manage to do all of this?"

Smiling, she set a hand on each of the kids' heads. "I had helpers." She peered down at them. "Both of whom also took very good naps."

He felt his eyes widen. "Again?" He and his mother were both guilty of giving in to Maddy's and Connor's claims that they weren't tired, and then allowing them to fall asleep on the couch. He hated fighting with them. And their cries always broke his heart.

"It's possible they were worn-out from helping me,"

said Alli, "but I simply told them they had to rest on their beds for an hour so their bodies could recharge."

"And they didn't argue?"

"No. I simply let them know what I expected from them."

Amazing.

"We had a good time. Now—" she looked down at the kids "—I need to get home for my own supper."

"You know you can stay, right?"

The hint of pink that crept into her cheeks gave him hope. "Yes, I do. And I will one day, perhaps."

Again the tangy aroma awakened his appetite. "What's for supper, anyway?"

"It's just something I threw together with whatever I could find. Some penne pasta in a meat sauce and some cheese. It's already cooked, just keeping warm in the oven. Oh, and I started a grocery list. It's there on the counter." She pointed beside the refrigerator. "I'm sure you'll want to add some things. But while I'm thinking about it, would you like me to do the grocery shopping, or would you prefer to do it yourself?"

"I'd hate to make you take the kids."

"Why? I think they'd enjoy the change of scenery. Though I would need their car seats."

Uncertainty had his brows lifting. "Are you sure? That hasn't been my experience. Matter of fact, it always seems to end up costing me more because they're always talking me into things that weren't on my list."

The air of mischief in her smile was a welcome sight. "That's because you're a soft touch."

He stiffened. "No, I'm not."

"When it comes to those two, yes, you are." Her expression softened. "But that's okay. I get it."

She'd pegged him, alright. Something she'd always

been good at. Yet seeing all she'd accomplished in one day had him feeling like he was failing his children. He was trying so hard to be both father and mother, in addition to running the ranch just as well as his dad had, that something always seemed to slip through the cracks. And in the end, he was failing at what mattered most.

"Jake?"

He met Alli's suddenly sober gaze.

"I wasn't criticizing you. My dad always was—and still is—a pushover where I'm concerned. It's okay."

"Yeah." The word came out on a chuckle, but he was cringing inside. Parenting wasn't one of those things you got a do-over on. It was one and done. And if he didn't get it right, it was Maddy and Connor who would ultimately pay the price for his failures.

Chapter Six

Alli maneuvered her Jeep up Jake's drive the next morning, still unable to shake the notion that she'd somehow hurt him with her comment about him being a soft touch. Even after he laughed off her apology, the way his eyes had darkened told her she'd struck a nerve. And for the life of her, she couldn't figure out why. There was nothing wrong with a father giving in to his children every now and then. And given that Jake was a single father, it was even more understandable.

Still, something about her offhanded remark had definitely bothered him, and that had bugged her all night, leading her to pray that he'd be in a better mood today.

Nearing the house, she spotted Jake on the porch, leaning against a post, one hand in his pocket while the other held a coffee mug as he watched her approach. Funny, he hadn't mentioned he wanted her to come early again. So why did he appear to be waiting on her? Watching for her? The way he used to.

The thought had an unwanted thrill skittering through her.

She promptly shook it off. Even if Jake had eagerly anticipated her arrival back in the day, it was only in anticipation of whatever they were planning to do. *Not* because of her.

After parking her Jeep alongside the house, she turned off the engine and got out, noting the same dismayed expression that had been on Jake's face when she left yesterday.

"I take it the kids are still asleep."

He nodded.

Continuing onto the porch, she said, "What's wrong?"

"Nothin'." Looking past her, he took another sip.

She crossed her arms over her chest and glared at him. "Well, I see it didn't take you long to go back on your promise."

His body went rigid, though he just continued to stare off into the distance without saying a word.

"Jake, you promised you'd be truthful with me. That was part of our deal. If you can't do that, then I'm out of here."

Like an inflatable bounce house with a leak, his body sagged. When he finally looked at her, she noticed the dark circles beneath his eyes.

"What's going on, Jake? Did I do something wrong?"

He puffed out a sarcastic laugh. "Hardly. You've gone above and beyond."

"So what's the problem?"

"Seeing everything you did yesterday made me realize how badly I've failed my children."

"What? How can you say that?"

He cast her a sideways glance. "Come on. You accomplished more in one day than I have in the last two months."

"So? You hired me to tend your children, keep up with the house and cook. That's all I did."

"Do you have any idea how long it's been since my

house has been this clean? I can't even remember the last time all the laundry was done."

"And now that it's caught up, you'll be able to stay on top of things with just a load every other day or so."

"You even rearranged stuff in the kitchen cabinets and the pantry."

"Yeah, well, my apartment was tiny, so I learned to make the most of any space."

"And I appreciate it. I really do." He winced then. "But I feel like a stranger in my own kitchen. I don't know where anything is anymore. I went to get a Moon-Pie out of the pantry last night and couldn't find them anywhere."

"Oh." She cringed, lowering her arms. "You must not eat them very often, then, because they expired six months ago, so I tossed them."

"Six months? Really?"

"You didn't notice that the chocolate was coated in white? Matter of fact, there were a lot of expired items in both the pantry and the refrigerator."

"See." He threw up his free hand as if she'd just confirmed everything he was saying. "Things I never would've noticed. My kids could've gotten botulism and it'd be all my fault."

She lifted a brow. "This is quite the pity party you've got going on here."

"Yeah, well, I was going to have some food to go with it, but apparently it's all spoiled." He stood there, staring into his coffee mug. "Now that I think about it, you always were a bit of a neat freak." He faced her again. "Are you sure you don't have a disorder or something?"

"*No.*" She straightened, hating the defensiveness in her voice. "I just prefer not to live like a slob."

"Did you just call me a slob?"

When the corners of his mouth twitched, she said, "If the shoe fits."

After a momentary stare down, they both laughed.

"Come on, I need some more coffee." He dumped the dregs from his cup before starting for the back door. "You know, for a moment there it felt like old times again."

"Yeah, it kinda did." And she wasn't sure how she felt about that.

He eyed her as they entered the kitchen. "Care for a cup?"

"Yes, please." She waited beside the island, watching as he opened two cupboards before locating the coffee cups.

After filling both mugs, he grabbed a second spoon from the drawer and cream from the refrigerator, then joined her at the island.

They doctored their morning beverages in silence, then sampled their efforts.

Meeting her gaze across the narrow space, Jake seemed to relax. "Okay, so the pantry and cupboards look great. I just need a map or something to help locate stuff. Do you think you can do that?"

"I already did." She moved to the pantry and opened the door. "Not a map, per se, but a list of items and where they're located." She pulled out the folded paper she'd tucked between two cans of soup yesterday, hoping he'd notice it. "I suppose I should've told you it was there."

He continued to watch her. "Let me guess. It's in alphabetical order?"

"For the most part."

He shook his head, then stared at her for a long moment, that muscle in his jaw twitching. "You always were smarter than me."

"That's why they called us Brainy and the Brawn." Though he had far more brawn now than back then.

He smiled in earnest, raising his cup. "I'd forgotten about that."

She closed the distance between them as he took a drink. "Jake?" She rested her palm on his forearm and waited for him to look at her. When he did, she said, "It's not a clean house, fancy meals at a perfectly set table or an organized pantry Maddy and Connor are going to remember when they grow up. It's bottle-feeding a calf, pulling weeds from the garden and all the other things they got to do with their father that will stay with them." His muscles tightened beneath her fingers.

He seemed to ponder her words. "I suppose you're right."

"No supposing about it." She pulled her hand away. "I *am* right. Because now that my mom is gone, it's those little things she and I did together that come to mind at the most unexpected times."

"Yeah, I know what you mean. Same with my dad." He reached for her hand. "Thank you, Alli. For everything."

"You're welcome." Turning, she retrieved the shopping list from beside the refrigerator and looked it over, noting that he'd added several things, including Moon-Pies. "Oh, I almost forgot. My dad and Francie are bringing back the annual Good Friday fish fry. You, the kids and your mom are all invited."

He nodded. "Your dad mentioned that at church Sunday. Then again yesterday when we were workin' cattle at Justin's."

Alli couldn't help laughing. "Yeah, they're both pretty

excited about it." After a moment, she eyed the list in her hand. "Now, if you wouldn't mind moving those car seats into my Jeep, the kids and I have an adventure to prepare for."

Jake lifted a skeptical brow. "Have you ever been grocery shopping with two toddlers before?"

She looked up at him. "No."

"It might be you who's in for the adventure, then." He downed the rest of his coffee. "Just sayin'."

An adventure with Maddy and Connor was fine by her. She was blessed that Jake had entrusted them to her care. If only everyone viewed children as the blessing they were, perhaps Lacy Hayes would still be alive.

Growing up, a Good Friday fish fry was tradition for both Jake's and Alli's families. They'd gather with the Prescotts, usually at Prescott Farms, and enjoy a day of food and fun. But the tradition ended after the death of Francie's first husband, Boyd, while Jake was at Sam Houston State. It marked the end of an era. Now here they were again, minus a few of the originals—Jake's dad, Alli's mom and Boyd—but hopefully reestablishing the event for the next generation.

Above-normal temperatures had everyone in shorts as they relaxed on Bill and Francie's patio, ceiling fans whirring overhead as they chatted about old times and Bill readied another round of catfish for the fryer. Maddy, Connor and Olivia danced around a small splash pad tucked beneath the large oak tree in the yard.

Annalise, Kyleigh and Alli had commandeered some squirt guns and took turns spritzing the kids, who never failed to squeal with glee. Jake couldn't help chuckling when Connor's eyes and mouth all rounded after a direct hit to his belly.

Jake's gaze drifted to Alli. After a rocky start to the week, they seemed to be settling into a rhythm. Her shopping trip with the kids had Alli confessing that it had been more challenging than she'd anticipated, though it hadn't seemed to deter her either. He was discovering a clean house really did make his life better. Keeping it clean wasn't nearly as challenging as letting it go and finding himself with a mountain of work. Not to mention how locating things was much easier.

Nonetheless, he was still in awe of how Alli seemed to do it all. Not just watching the kids, but teaching and engaging them, making sure they had fun—all the while keeping a clean house and always having meals ready and waiting.

Today, though, he was hoping to snag a few minutes alone with her. To have a conversation that didn't revolve around the kids or his house. To enjoy each other's company the way they used to.

A stream of icy water hit his neck, jolting him from his reverie.

He looked up to see Alli standing a few feet away, mischief lifting the corners of her mouth.

Two could play at that game.

Willing himself to remain calm, he stood, his gaze trained on her. "You think that's funny, huh?"

Dressed in cutoffs and a tank top, she giggled like a schoolgirl and took aim again, hitting him smack-dab in the middle of his chest, the moisture quickly soaking through his T-shirt.

He looked from his shirt to her. "This means war."

Alli bolted as he reached for the soaker gun someone had left on the table.

"I don't know whose this is," he said, "but I'm borrowing it." He checked to make sure it had water in it, then took off in the direction Alli had gone. Until his instincts had him doing an about-face. She expected him to come after her. So while she continued around the house, he'd go the opposite direction and wait for her to come to him.

Moments later, he was on the near end of the house, peering around the corner. Sure enough, she was tip-toeing his way, periodically glancing over her shoulder.

Slipping out of sight, he pumped the water cannon a couple of times and waited.

Her gaze was still trained behind her when she came into view.

"Let's see how funny you think it is." Not wanting to make her mad, he aimed for her legs while she danced a jig, squealing like a girl.

He paused, a morsel of satisfaction revealing itself in a smile. "Had enough?"

She glared at him, her chest rising and falling in rapid succession. "That is so not fair."

"Oh, and your unprovoked attack was?"

"Point taken." She grinned. "But the look on your face was priceless."

"I could say the same thing." He couldn't seem to stop smiling. In that all-too-brief moment, they were kids again. Besties, as she used to say. And he liked it.

"All right, you two." His mother's voice echoed behind him. "Dry off and come eat."

Over supper, the topic of conversation revolved around Hawkins and Annalise's wedding next weekend. And as usual, there was far too much food. Naturally, Jake sampled every last bit of it.

Pushing his plate away, he stood, patting his bloated midsection. He'd eaten way too much. But everything was so good.

"Francie, you've outdone yourself."

"Thank you, Jake. I'm glad you liked it."

"A little too much, I'm afraid."

"Do what I do, then," said Bill. "Walk it off and come back for more." He chuckled.

Even Alli had eaten more than her fair share. Or so she said. She'd gone to her apartment a few minutes ago, stating that she needed to change into some stretchy shorts. Maybe he could convince her to take a walk with him.

He glanced at Maddy, sitting with Kyleigh, watching something on the teen's phone and giggling.

Connor and Olivia had found their way back to the splash pad and Annalise had turned the water back on.

"You know, a walk isn't a bad idea." Jake eyed his mother who was still at the table. "Would you mind keeping an eye on Maddy and Connor?"

"Of course not, Jakey. I haven't seen them all week." Noting where each child was at the moment, she waved him on. "They'll be fine. You go for your walk."

"Thanks, Mom."

He started toward the far end of the house so it wouldn't be obvious that he was headed to Alli's apartment. Though as he rounded the corner, he saw her coming down the steps.

"Hey."

She turned at the sound of his voice. "You going somewhere?"

"Taking a little walk, hoping to wear off some of this food." He massaged his stomach.

"I know what you mean. I'm feeling rather bloated myself."

"Why don't you join me, then?" When she hesitated, he added, "My mom is keeping an eye on the kids." Realizing how that sounded, he promptly added, "Not that I was expecting you to watch them."

There was an air of sadness in her eyes when she looked up at him. "Actually, a walk would be nice. Thank you."

The sun had begun its slow descent toward the western horizon as they moved away from the house and toward the copse of oak trees where Alli once had a tree house. They used to hang out in that thing for hours.

Keeping pace with her as they strode through the grass, he got the sense that something was wrong. "Are you okay?"

She shrugged. "It's just me being emotional. No big deal."

"Alli, if something's bothering you, in my book, that's a big deal." Reaching for her elbow, he stepped in front of her. "What's going on?"

She looked everywhere but at him. Then, with another shrug, she said, "It's just that the last time we all got together like this, my mom was with us."

The sudden realization had him wincing. "And this was her house."

Alli lowered her gaze, nodding. "Don't get me wrong. I don't begrudge Dad or Francie for wanting to bring back the fish fry. I'm glad they did it. It was fun. I just got a little melancholy, that's all."

Thoughts of his father had come to mind more than once today, too. But his mom seemed to be handling things okay, so he'd sloughed it off.

Tucking his hands in the pockets of his golf shorts to keep from pulling her into his arms, he said, "Kinda strange, how things have changed."

Her smile was a sad one. "And yet so many of the players are still the same."

"How did you feel when you found out about your dad and Francie?"

Once again picking her way through the grass, she said, "Actually, I was happy for him. He was so sad after Mama died. It's hard to lose someone you love. Especially when you've been together for a long time. You find yourself floundering, wondering how you're supposed to move on without them." Stopping, she looked up at him. "I guess you can understand that, huh? Losing your wife so suddenly."

He couldn't help the sigh that escaped. If she only knew.

"Would you think I'm a horrible person if I said I wasn't the grieving widower most people would've expected?"

Her brow puckered in confusion and suddenly he felt the urge to be released from the secret he'd held on to for so long.

You promised you'd be truthful with her.

He sucked in a breath. "Before Bethany left the house the day of her accident, she told me she wanted a divorce. Said she'd found someone else. We argued. Then, as she walked out the door, she said she deserved someone who cared more about her than some stupid cattle."

Alli winced. "Ouch."

"I was so angry. I wanted her to feel the same kind of pain I was feeling. Then, a couple hours later, while I was still stewing, feeling sorry for myself, my phone rang. A guy I used to know when I was on the force informed me she was gone. Someone had been weaving in and out of traffic and clipped her vehicle. Witnesses said she overcorrected and slammed into a concrete wall." He cleared the thickness in his throat. "I've never told anyone about our argument. Until now."

"Not even your mother?"

He shook his head.

Compassion filled Alli's pretty eyes. "You know, it's not healthy to hold everything in like that."

He shrugged. "I was too embarrassed to tell anyone."

"Why? Bethany made her choices."

"Yes, but I wasn't innocent. From the day we moved out here, I was so busy trying to fill all the vacancies left by my dad that I guess it blinded me to what was truly important. I failed them all. My dad, my wife, my kids. Now here I am trying to fill the vacancies left by Bethany. And failing once more." He stared into the trees, afraid to meet Alli's gaze for fear he'd see her sympathy. He wasn't sure he could bear that.

"Jake, none of us can be everything to everyone. That's why God gave us all different gifts." He felt her fingers press into his arm. "I'm sorry for what Bethany did to you. But you only need to be you."

Looking from her hand to her face, he said, "What if that's not enough?"

"Then your weakness is the perfect canvas for God to display His strength. When we are weak, He is strong."

"Easier said than done."

"Yeah, I know." Lowering her hand, she walked away. But not before he saw the pain in her eyes, pain that went beyond what he'd just told her. "Failure is never easy to accept. Especially when it impacts the lives of others."

Confused, he caught up to her in two swift strides. "Alli, I can't imagine you failing at anything."

"In that case, you would be quite wrong." She stopped, staring out over the rolling hills, her expression tormented. "I left CPS after one of my cases died at the hands of her addict father."

Hearing the pain in her voice, he waited while she struggled to continue.

"Despite my recommendations that the child remain in foster care, a visiting judge ruled otherwise. Less than a month later, the father went into a drug-induced rage. His wife was severely injured while the child…" Alli lifted her tear-filled eyes to the tree limbs, blinking rapidly.

Jake couldn't help the groan that escaped as he reached for her hand. "And you're blaming yourself, even though you know you're not responsible."

Her simple nod had him longing to pull her into his arms. And it took every ounce of energy not to do it.

Instead, he stroked her soft knuckles with his calloused thumb. "I'm so sorry, Alli. It was the judge who failed that child, though, not you."

"I know that in here." She tapped the side of her head. "But in here—" she gestured to her heart "—it feels very personal."

"You can't help second-guessing, thinking there was something more you could've done, right?" Kind of like him.

She nodded again.

"As a former police officer, I get it. I'm sure we've both seen some things we wish we could unsee." He sighed, longing to take away her pain. "There's a whole lotta bad in this world, isn't there?"

"There sure is." She swiped at a tear that managed to slip past her defenses.

He pretended not to notice. "Just for the record, I'm thankful my children have you looking after them. I trust you, Alli. And that's not something I take lightly."

"I don't either. And I promise you, I will do everything in my power to keep them safe."

Chapter Seven

What had started out as a simple walk ended up dramatically shifting Jake's perspective.

By the time he and Alli rejoined the others Friday night, Jake felt as though every last ounce of energy had left his body. And perhaps it had.

Your weakness is the perfect canvas for God to display His strength.

Alli was right. God was at work. Jake had never realized just how tightly he'd been clinging to the knowledge of Bethany's betrayal until he opened up to Alli about it the other night. This whole time, he'd been placing all the blame for the breakdown of his marriage on Bethany, convincing himself he was innocent. Yet as he spoke the words aloud for the first time, it was as though he was looking at things through a different lens. One that revealed his own transgressions. And it had been humbling, to say the least.

Since then, he'd been doing a lot of soul-searching. Instead of working over the weekend, he'd focused solely on the kids, save for riding out to check cattle. Even then, the kids enjoyed getting to ride on the utility vehicle.

Then as he listened to Pastor speak Sunday morning, Jake realized anew how that first Easter had changed everything. Because of Jesus's death—and more importantly, His resurrection—the debt for our sins had been paid. And if God could forgive Jake for everything he'd ever done, then who was he not to forgive Bethany? Especially when she wasn't the only one responsible for the breakdown of their marriage.

By the time Alli arrived this morning, he felt as though a weight had been lifted. Apparently, she'd noticed something, too, commenting about how well rested he appeared.

Now, as he parked the utility vehicle in the shade of twin mulberry trees dwarfed by towering oaks and loblolly pines, he savored the peace he'd always found at the old swimming hole. Lifting his hat, he dragged a hand through his hair while a breeze rustled the leaves and sent ripples dancing across the water.

When he and Bethany first moved out here, she'd been almost giddy. Having lived her whole life in the city, she embraced the change in lifestyle. While she spent her days overseeing the renovation of the house, he was consumed with running the ranch, trying to live up to the example his father had set. Yet while the renovations came to an end, ranch work was a constant, meaning his routine remained the same.

With Bethany's family in Houston, Jake had foolishly assumed she'd make friends in Hope Crossing. But that had never really happened. Throw in the fact that she'd left the workforce right before Maddy was born and, well, Bethany spent most days at home alone, caring for the kids while Jake did whatever he thought had to be done.

Then, suddenly, Bethany was gone, and Jake was forced to pull back on his work to be with his children.

It wasn't the first time it had cost him someone he loved to realize what was truly important.

Stepping out of the machine, he lifted his face to scan the trees. Spotting an overabundance of green berries, he smiled as fond memories played through his mind. To his knowledge, Alli had yet to bring the kids down here. She'd be pleased to hear there would be plenty of mulberries this year.

Lowering his gaze, he stared out over the water, recalling all the fun he and Alli used to have here when they were kids. Before he destroyed their friendship. Something he'd taken for granted, just like he had Bethany.

He closed his eyes. *Forgive me, Lord, for failing to appreciate two of the greatest gifts You've ever given me. For assuming they'd always be there and that the bond we shared was unbreakable. I was selfish. Probably still am.*

Thank You for bringing Alli back into my life and into the lives of my children. Help me be the friend she needs and to not mess things up again. In Jesus' name, amen.

Lifting his gaze, he felt the sun on his face as he drew in a deep breath. And for the first time since Bethany stormed out of his life, he felt his heart beat again.

He glanced at his watch before hopping back into the utility vehicle. Alli probably had supper almost ready, so he'd best get on home.

Making a U-turn toward the house, he found himself wishing Alli would hang around awhile instead of running off as soon as he got there. Their walk Friday evening had reiterated how much he'd missed her friendship. And he would continue to do whatever it took to prove himself worthy of it once again.

When he reached the house several minutes later, Alli and the kids were outside, watering their garden.

"Daddy!" Maddy bounded toward him.

He swooped her into his arms, continuing to thank God for both her and Connor. As well as the woman he'd entrusted with their care. "How was your day?"

"Good. We went to the library and Alli read to all the kids." Maddy wriggled to get down. Then bolted toward Alli as Connor latched on to Jake's legs.

Lifting his son, he kissed the boy's chubby cheek, noting his T-shirt was damp. "Were you helping Miss Alli water the plants?"

Connor nodded, his smile wide as he twisted to watch his sister take over the hose.

Still holding Connor, Jake moved alongside Alli. "So, you're taking your reading show on the road now, huh?"

She waved him off with a chuckle. "I simply was reading to Maddy and Connor when another mom came in with two little ones. Next thing I knew, my audience had doubled."

"I get the feeling you enjoy reading to them as much as they like listening to you. Who knows where that could lead."

"Yeah right, Walker." She gave him a playful shove.

"What? I'm serious."

A ringtone echoed from the back pocket of Allie's jeans. She retrieved the phone, a mixture of curiosity and something else pinching her expression when she looked at the screen.

"Excuse me." Turning away, she tapped the screen before putting the phone to her ear. "Hello." She meandered away, making it impossible for him to hear anything more.

Focusing on Maddy again, he noticed puddles forming around the plants. "I think they've had enough for now, Madikins." He set Connor to the ground before moving to the spigot to turn off the water.

Still holding the now-dripping nozzle, his daughter frowned. "But I wasn't done."

"We don't want to drown the plants." He cast another glance in Alli's direction.

She must've seen him, because she hollered, "Y'all go on in. I'll be there shortly."

Noting the sudden drop of her shoulders and the way she raked her free hand through her hair, he wasn't too keen on the idea, but decided she deserved her privacy. No matter how badly he wanted to know who was on the other end of that phone.

Inside the house, the unmistakable aroma of roast beef washed over him. He breathed deeply, hoping there were some mashed potatoes to go with it. Not that he'd complain if there weren't. He appreciated everything Alli did and was going to make sure she knew it. But how?

Continuing into the kitchen, he determined to come up with something.

"Can I watch a pony show?" Maddy perched a hand on her hip.

Peering out the window, Jake saw Alli was still on the phone.

"Pony sow," Connor echoed.

Jake tore his gaze from the window. "I suppose that'll be alright. But just one episode."

No sooner had he gotten the kids settled than Alli rushed into the kitchen.

"I need to get these rolls into the oven." She punched a couple buttons on the stove.

"No hurry." He crossed from the living room into the kitchen, noting her jerky movements. "Are you okay?"

"Yeah." The word came out too quickly. She grabbed the lid on the Crock-Pot, only to have it clatter onto the counter.

Moving beside her, Jake took hold of her elbow and stared at her. "I don't know who you were on the phone with, but something's got you rattled. And since you don't rattle easily…" Even though he wanted to say more, to push her to tell him who she'd been talking to, he simply waited.

For a brief moment, she closed her eyes and took a deep breath.

Giving her elbow a gentle squeeze, he said, "Why don't you go sit down while I get you a glass of tea."

To his surprise, she didn't argue. Simply nodded and moved to the table.

He grabbed two mason jars, added some ice, then filled them with tea, noting that the kids were still engrossed in their show. After setting the drinks on the table, he moved another chair beside Alli's. "You don't have to tell me anything if you don't want to. But if you need to talk, I'm here."

She nodded, then took a couple gulps of tea. "Thank you."

"You're welcome."

Finally, she met his gaze, puffing out a chuckle. "I'm sorry to worry you. I'm being ridiculous."

He lifted a brow, still longing to know who had called her. "The Alli I know is never ridiculous."

"That was my ex-fiancé." She took another sip. "Emphasis on *ex*."

Unable to stop himself, he said, "In other words, the jerk who left you high and dry a week before your wedding."

Her smile turned shy. "Also known as Travis."

"I'm dying to know what prompted him to call you now." He hoped the guy wasn't trying to get back into Alli's good graces. Not after what he'd done to her.

Fingering the condensation on her glass, she shrugged. "He wanted to let me know he's getting married."

Jake felt his jaw drop. "Seriously? What kind of guy does that? Was he just trying to rub salt in the wound or what?"

"No, he was doing me a courtesy before it went all over social media."

"Courtesy?"

She held up a hand. "Before you come down on him too hard, you should know I'm glad Travis had the courage to break things off, because I probably would've been miserable."

"And why is that?"

"Because I loved the idea of being married more than I loved him. Matter of fact, I'm not sure I ever really loved Travis. As a friend, perhaps, but not romantically. Thankfully, he was smart enough to recognize that."

"Okay, but couldn't he have done it sooner? And why would you want to marry someone you didn't love?"

Again, she stared at her glass. "Because he loved me. I knew he'd be good to me. And, if I'm being truly honest—" she looked at him now "—I was tired of being alone."

Jake simply stared. "Why would you shortchange yourself like that, Alli? You're a vibrant, beautiful woman with a lot of love to give."

"I'm also a bit jaded."

Jake felt as though he'd been punched in the gut. He took a swig of tea to chase away the sudden lump in his throat. "I don't want this to sound arrogant or anything, but I suppose I played a role in that, huh?"

She simply shrugged.

"Oh, no. Don't you go shrugging me off, Alli Krenek." Resting one elbow on the table, he leaned closer. "You expect me to be honest with you. So show me the same courtesy."

"Okay, fine!" She hesitated. "Maybe."

"Maybe what?"

"*Maybe* you had something to do with it." With a sigh, she continued. "I don't know. I had so many insecurities when I was younger. You were the only one I could be myself with. You knew me inside and out and accepted me just the way I was."

"Until I chose to let the voices of my so-called friends overrule my heart." How many lives had he impacted with his stupid, selfish decisions?

God, forgive me. Help me make this right. Somehow. Some way.

"I can't seem to say it enough, Alli, but I'm sorry. I knew I was hurting you even as I said those awful words. I just never realized how much." His heart ached something fierce. "To make matters worse, I never recognized how special you were to me until it was too late." He reached for her hand. "I know I don't deserve it, but can you ever forgive me?"

She stared at him, her expression somber. "No, Jake."

His entire being cringed. He started to release her hand, but she squeezed tighter.

"Because I already have. That day I finally heard you apologize."

Thank You, God.

"You have no idea how much that means to me, Alli."

She watched him. "Yeah, I think I do." Standing, she said, "I need to get the rolls in the oven." After crossing to the counter, she lifted the plastic wrap from a pan of yeast rolls. Suddenly her movement slowed. "Since my dad and Francie are meeting some friends for dinner in Brenham tonight, would you mind if I stayed for supper?" The uncharacteristically shy expression on her face nearly took his breath away.

He couldn't help smiling. "Alli, you are always welcome at our table."

After all he'd done, he did not deserve to have this woman in his life again. But he was so glad she was. And while he could easily fall for Alli all over again, he'd best keep things in the friend zone. Because if he didn't, he'd risk her walking away once again.

And he wasn't sure he could bear that.

With the wedding photos complete, Hawkins's and Annalise's families moved into the barn at the Christmas tree farm Saturday evening, while Alli lingered near the floral-covered arch that had served as an altar, basking in the glow of the setting sun. What was the likelihood that Travis would call her mere days before she attended someone else's wedding? That was so like him, though, to let her know he was engaged. Not to be spiteful, but because his tenderhearted soul always considered other people's feelings.

Yet another reason why she'd been too cowardly to break things off, despite not loving him the way a woman should love the man she was going to marry.

Not that she was an expert. She'd only been in love once. Or thought she was, anyway. As if her teen self had really known what love was. At thirty-four, she still wasn't sure. She could only hope she'd recognize it if it ever happened again. That spark that Hawkins and Annalise shared. Not just now, as they'd pledged their lives to one another, but anytime they were together. There was an obvious glimmer that made it plain to everyone around them that they belonged together.

With Travis, there'd never been any spark. And truth be known, that was what Alli wanted. Or maybe all-out fireworks.

She let go a sigh and started toward the red pole barn. A girl could dream. Of course, first she'd have to find the courage to open her heart so fully to someone that her feelings couldn't be contained.

At the entrance to the barn, Alli paused. She'd been thrilled when Annalise requested her help in decorating the barn for the reception. Felt like she belonged when Annalise personally invited her to last night's rehearsal and dinner. And then honored to be present as the bride prepared to walk down the aisle. But stepping into the reception with no one on her arm had Alli feeling apprehensive.

Forcing herself to take a deep breath, she smoothed a shaky hand over her pale purple sleeveless sheath dress and scanned the interior of the space that had been transformed with hundreds of lights and yards of sheer white fabric draped from the rafters. They'd done a good job of bringing Annalise's dream to life. Rustic elegance was what she'd been going for and the white tablecloth-covered round tables, with centerpieces consisting of white pillar candles nestled among Leyland cypress boughs from the tree farm with just a touch of eucalyptus and mercury glass votive holders for contrast, had achieved just that.

Chatter filled the comfortable evening air spilling

through the open doors and windows, all but drowning out the country tunes playing low on the deejay's speakers alongside the dance floor. White folding screens to her left still concealed the seemingly endless charcuterie board that boasted an abundance of meats, cheeses, fruits, nuts, vegetables, breads and more. The spread was like a treasure trove just waiting to be explored. If only anxiety didn't have her stomach in a headlock.

To her right, near the back, she spotted some members of her Sunday school class seated together. Yet while she recognized a few of them, she'd been gone for so long, she didn't really know anyone anymore. Except Jake.

After visually locating the long table where the family was to sit, Alli eyed the beverage table holding large acrylic containers filled with tea—sweetened and unsweetened—lemonade and water. She started that way and was met by a member of the catering team, a young woman wearing a bright smile atop her black-and-white attire.

"Would you care for a drink, ma'am?" she asked.

Alli cringed. *Ma'am*? She wasn't old enough to be a ma'am yet, was she? Then she glanced at the server who looked as though she was barely old enough to babysit. "Lemonade, please." Her hands fidgeted as the woman reached for a clear plastic cup. "On second thought, make that water." At the rate Alli was going, she was apt to spill something on her dress.

"Miss Alli!"

She wobbled on her four-inch heels as Maddy threw her arms around Alli's legs with all the exuberance of a four-year-old.

"Easy there, Madikins." A smiling Jake trailed his daughter, carrying Connor. "You'll knock her over."

Alli felt heat creeping into her cheeks when he touched her elbow.

"You okay?"

Despite the heels, she still had to look up to meet his gaze. "Yeah." She'd barely gotten the word out when Connor lunged for her. As she reached to intercept him, Jake's free arm slid around her waist. He tugged her close, holding her steady as another surge of warmth swept over her.

"Dude?" Frowning at his son, Jake relaxed his hold on Alli. "You need to stop doing that. If you want Miss Alli to hold you, you need to ask her first."

Connor's bottom lip pooched out, making Alli forget her insecurities.

She hugged him closer. "Aww, how could I turn down such sweet snuggles?"

"Your water." The server passed her the cup.

"I can take that." Jake intercepted the drink. "We have an extra seat, if you'd like to join us."

Only then did Alli get a good look at him. And promptly wished she hadn't. To say Jake cleaned up well was an understatement. He'd obviously pulled out all the stops for his friend's wedding. His hair had been trimmed and he was clean-shaven. The light blue button-down that drew attention to his eyes topped a pair of khaki dress pants. He'd even shined his Sunday-go-to-meetin' boots.

But it was more than his physical appearance that captured her attention. Alli couldn't put her finger on it, but something about Jake had changed. Ever since they took that walk at the fish fry, he'd been…different. Not in any dramatic way, just little things like having her coffee ready and waiting when she arrived each morning. Then sticking around to share a cup with her while they talked about whatever was at the forefront of their minds on any given day. Thanking her before she left, and then watching her drive off until she was out of sight.

"There you are, Alli." Francie moved in front of them, looking lovely in a short-sleeved, blue-gray dress with a flowing skirt. "I don't mean to interrupt, I just wanted to let you know that your dad and I saved a seat for you." She glanced at Jake then, the corners of her mouth lifting even more. "That is, unless you have other plans." With a wink, she scurried away.

Alli cleared her throat, wishing she could hide under the beverage table. "Well, that wasn't awkward at all."

"Probably why she gets along so well with my mother," said Jake.

Maddy peered up at her. "Pleeeeeze sit by me."

Sitting with Jake's children would certainly keep Alli occupied. But she didn't want Annalise and Hawkins to feel slighted either. They'd gone out of their way to make her feel like one of the family. But there, too, she'd be the odd man out. The only single tucked among a bunch of couples.

Yet sitting with Jake could pose a different problem—like people assuming they were together.

And people thought small towns provided a simpler way of life.

Connor set a hand on each of Alli's cheeks, his expression serious. "Peeze?"

Her heart was now a puddle on the floor. How could she possibly say no to that?

She touched her nose to his. "Okay."

Thankfully, Joanna was also at the table, so they each had a child between them. But that meant Alli was smack-dab in the middle, as close to Jake as she was to Joanna, instead of having a three-person buffer like she'd hoped for. But once folks settled in to eat, Dottie Rodgers and her husband, Willard, joined them, helping to keep the conversation lively.

Before long, the bride and groom were sharing their first dance, followed by the mother/son and father/daughter dances.

Suddenly, Alli's father appeared at her side. He extended his hand. "Care to join me, sweetheart?"

Tears sprang to her eyes. She hadn't expected this.

Blinking rapidly, she set her hand in his calloused one. "Of course, Daddy."

He led her to the dance floor before pulling her into those strong arms that had always been her haven. Then she realized what song was playing: Celine Dion's "Because You Loved Me." The same song they would've danced to at her wedding, had it actually happened.

"Were you feeling left out?" With her right hand in his and her left hand on his shoulder, she looked up at her father.

"Perhaps." His blue-green eyes held her gaze. "We missed our opportunity last year."

She couldn't help thinking of her wedding that never was. The one she'd painstakingly planned down to every detail, then had to cancel. Bless his heart, Travis even helped her pay all the fees.

Why had she been planning such a lavish wedding anyway? That was so not her.

"Daddy." She smoothed a hand over the lapel of his jacket. "What if I'm incapable of loving?"

He cast her a bewildered look. "What do you mean incapable? You're one of the most loving people I know."

"That's not what I mean, and you know it. Travis loved me. He was a good man. But I didn't love him back."

The man shook his head. "Alli, my darlin', just because Travis wasn't the right one doesn't mean there isn't someone else out there for you. You know, with your mama, I knew she was the one I was going to spend my life with the first time I laid eyes on her. But with Francie, we were just friends. We kept each other company. Then, out of the blue, somethin' sparked."

Alli couldn't help smiling. Francie had made her father happy again.

Touching a finger to her chin, her father coaxed her to look at him. "I don't know what God has planned for you, baby girl. But I pray that if He does send love your way, you'll embrace it instead of second-guessing it to death. Love is never perfect. And it ain't easy. It requires a lot of hard work and a humble heart. But when it's right, it's worth it."

The music shifted and as the sound of a fiddle filled the air with the unmistakable notes of "Cotton-Eyed Joe," whoops and hollers went up all over the space.

"We'd better get out of the way." She tugged her father off the dance floor, only to have someone take hold of her other arm.

"Oh, no you don't."

She looked up to see a smiling Jake.

"They're playin' our song." The way he waggled his eyebrows made her laugh.

She'd been in tenth grade, him in eleventh, when she'd taught him how to dance the Cotton-Eyed Joe. They'd spent months practicing in her daddy's barn for a contest that was to take place at the dance at the Hope Crossing Fair and Rodeo that year. Jake hadn't had an ounce of rhythm to his name, so it had been an uphill battle. But when they placed that trophy in their hands at the end of the dance, it had been worth all the pain and agony.

"I don't know how much kicking I can do in this straight skirt," she said, "but I'll give it a go."

He slipped an arm around her waist, and she did the same with him as the bride and groom came alongside them to form a quartet. Arm in arm in a line, they moved forward and back, kicking, scootin' and having a ball. Then the song morphed into Brooks and Dunn's "Boot Scootin' Boogie" and Jake pulled her into his arms for some two-steppin'.

She lifted a brow. "You do realize I'm wearing heels."

A smile tugged at his lips. His hold tightened as he looked into her eyes. "Don't worry, I've got you, Alli. I won't let you fall."

An awareness that hadn't been there before sifted through her. Something terrifying and exhilarating at the same time. Because in that moment, she saw Jake for the man he'd become instead of the boy she still thought him to be. And that spelled danger with a capital *D*.

Chapter Eight

Pure enjoyment. That was the only way to describe what Jake had felt at Hawkins and Annalise's reception. He wasn't sure he could even recall the last time he'd smiled and laughed so much. For the first time since Bethany's death, he'd felt like his old self again. Now that it was over, though, things had become awkward.

Saturday night it was almost as if he and Alli were a couple, instead of just friends. Yeah, he knew he needed to keep things on a friends-only basis, but boy, that had sure been difficult when he saw the way a couple of the other guys had looked at her. They were intrigued, to say the least. And who could blame them?

Alli was the kind of woman who wasn't afraid to get her hands dirty. She was tough. Almost to a fault. But she was also gentle. Caring. And when she decided to pull out the stops and go all feminine the way she'd done the other night, well, she was downright irresistible.

But while he'd spent the entire evening telling himself he was simply looking out for her well-being, he knew better. Despite the fact that he had absolutely no right, he felt possessive when it came to Alli. Always had. Except the other night was different. There was a longing that had him sticking close to her. The same one that had urged him to ask her out all those years ago.

And look how that turned out.

No way could he let that happen again. He needed to rein in his foolish notions and remember that Alli was his employee and friend, nothing more. So as he approached his house in the utility vehicle just before suppertime Monday, he knew he wouldn't be inviting Alli to stay the way he had so many times before. If he planned to keep things strictly business, he couldn't afford it.

His phone chimed as he passed the barn. After awkwardly tugging it from the pocket of his worn Wranglers, he glanced at the screen. Ted Galloway.

Jake's gut tightened. While he'd always had a good relationship with his in-laws, things had been awkward since Bethany's death. Withholding the truth from Ted and Brenda had him feeling guilty. Even though he knew it would wound them deeply. Ted was a former pastor. How could Jake tell him his daughter had been having an affair? What if Ted didn't believe him? That could cause a rift that might end up impacting Maddy and Connor in a negative way.

After killing the engine, he answered the call. "Hey, Ted. How's it going?" Somehow, he'd fake his way through what he hoped would be a short conversation.

"Not too bad. How are things out your way? Kids doing alright?"

"Everything's fine. They have a new nanny."

"That's fantastic news. I know you've been hoping to find someone. Brenda and I will look forward to meeting this person."

Jake wasn't expecting that. And though he wasn't sure why, the notion had him shifting in his seat.

After a brief pause, Ted continued. "We heard there's a new drive-through wildlife park not too far from Hope Crossing. Thought, if it's alright with you, we'd come out there Saturday and take the kids to visit it."

Meaning Jake would have to see Bethany's folks. Talk with them. But then, it wasn't like he could say no. He'd promised himself he'd never keep the kids from them. That would not only be selfish, but just plain wrong.

"I'm sure they'd love that."

"Great. We'll head out first thing Saturday morning, then, so we should be there to pick them up around nine thirty."

"Sounds good, Ted. The kids will be excited."

"See you Saturday."

Jake repocketed his phone, his insides knotting. The only thing worse than talking on the phone with Bethany's parents was seeing them face-to-face, pretending Jake and Bethany had had the perfect marriage. Jake hadn't been foolish enough to believe that even prior to Bethany's demand for a divorce.

He restarted the UTV and continued on to the house, wishing he could talk the situation over with Alli. She was the only person who knew the whole story. But he'd already decided to let her go on home. Given his mood, that was probably for the best. Maybe they could talk in the morning.

As he brought the vehicle to a halt near the rear of the house, the back door flew open, and both kids and dogs bounded toward him. After closing the door, Alli followed, her smile wide.

The sight lifted his spirits.

Beast barked as Jake stepped out of the vehicle while

Beauty nudged his hand for a quick rub. Maddy and Connor stopped in front of him, their smiles wide.

Maddy peered up at him, squinting against the sun. "We're going to have a picnic for supper, Daddy."

"A picnic?" His confused gaze trailed to Alli as she approached.

"At the library this morning—" she stopped behind the kids "—we read a book about a picnic, and they've been talking about it ever since. So with this beautiful weather—" she waved a hand through the air "—I went ahead and prepared a picnic supper." Pulling her bottom lip between her teeth, she lifted a shoulder. "I hope you don't mind."

His brain was having a hard time shifting gears. "Are you suggesting we just eat it out here?" He motioned to the wooden picnic table beneath an oak tree.

"Actually—" Alli's hope-filled smile had him hanging on her every word "—I thought the swimming hole would be a nice setting."

"Oh." Once again, his mind took off down memory lane. How many times had he and Alli picnicked there as kids? They'd each bring a lunch and hang out there until they were waterlogged, sunburned and thoroughly exhausted. Or caught their share of fish.

"I reckon the kids would get a kick out of that."

"Miss Alli said she'd go, too." Maddy bounced up and down.

The one time he was ready to send her on her way.

"*If* you don't mind," she was quick to inject.

Another set of eyes to watch the kids around the water would be good, he supposed.

"After you went to all that trouble? Of course you should come."

Her smile grew wider. "In that case, I'll go grab our supper."

While she did that, he helped the kids don their rubber boots.

Soon, the bed of the UTV was loaded with his mother's barely used picnic basket, an insulated drink container and an old quilt, and they were on their way with Beauty and Beast running alongside them.

Just as he'd done on his last trip to the fishing hole, he parked beneath the mulberry trees.

Maddy hurried toward the water's edge, her brother on her heels. "Daddy, we have a lake?"

The surprise in her voice was hard to miss.

"Have they not been here before?" Alli unfurled the quilt midway between their vehicle and the water.

"It's been a while." Before Bethany died, actually. Jake shook his head. No wonder Maddy didn't remember.

As Connor squatted to peer into the water, Jake joined them. "Careful, buddy. I'd hate for you to fall in." Not that it was very deep. But still.

"Wook! Shish!" The boy giggled, pointing to the minnows darting back and forth in the shallow water.

It did Jake's heart good to see his kids so happy. And, once again, he had Alli to thank.

"Would you like to eat or explore first?" He turned at the sound of Alli's voice to find her standing behind him, hands tucked in her back pockets.

Looking past her, he saw their picnic was all set up. "I reckon we should ask these two." Setting a hand atop each of his children's heads, he said, "Do y'all want to eat now or explore first?"

"Eat!" Maddy was quick to respond.

"I eat, too." As usual, Connor went along with whatever his sister suggested.

As the kids hurried toward the blanket, Alli snagged the sleeve of Jake's work shirt, preventing his retreat. "I get the impression you're not all that enthused about our little picnic."

"What?" He forced a smile. "No. I'm just surprised, that's all. I wasn't expecting it."

"Sometimes a little spontaneity can be good." She studied him with those eyes that seemed to see right through him. "And I'm saying that as much to myself as I am to you." She took a step closer. "Does this distance I'm sensing from you have anything to do with Saturday night?"

After all these years, she still knew him too well. At least the reception wasn't the only thing on his mind.

Hands on his hips, he shook his head. "My father-in-law called while I was on my way to the house."

"Hurry, Daddy." Maddy dropped to her knees beside the picnic basket.

He let go a sigh. "Look, I don't want to ruin the kids' fun. Let's get them fed, then we can talk."

"I'm gonna hold you to it. Because you look like you could use a friend."

A friend. Despite his heart's urging, that was all she could ever be.

It didn't take them long to devour their meal of pulled pork sandwiches, carrot sticks, potato chips and oatmeal raisin cookies. Jake was surprised how much the kids ate. More than usual. Either they'd worked up an appetite, or perhaps he should consider this picnic thing more often.

When they'd finished their meal, Alli showed Maddy and Connor the mulberries that still had a couple of weeks before they'd be ready to pick. Then they followed the children and both dogs as they returned to the water to watch the minnows.

"For as much as you always loved to fish, I'm surprised you haven't gotten them poles yet." Alli nodded toward the kids.

"They were both so young when Bethany died, I guess it seemed a little daunting. But I suppose they're getting old enough now."

She shrugged. "As long as they have life jackets, they'll be fine. It's not that deep along here."

"Perhaps I'll check out their rods next time I'm at Plowman's."

Her gaze still fixed on the kids, she leaned closer. "What did your father-in-law have to say that got you so wound up?"

Jake sucked in a breath. "They want to see the kids this weekend. Take them to that—" he leaned closer and lowered his voice "—new wildlife park."

Her eyes widened. "They'll love that."

"I know."

"So what's the problem?"

He briefly explained how withholding things from his in-laws made him uncomfortable. "Our conversations just aren't the same. They aren't genuine because I'm so afraid I'm going to let something slip."

"Since I'm the only one you've ever told, I doubt that would happen. But I understand why you wouldn't want to tell them. You don't want to taint their daughter's memory."

"Yeah." The word came out on a sigh.

She placed a hand on his shoulder, and it was as if he could feel her compassion seeping into his bones. "That's very admirable, Jake."

Coming from anyone else, those words probably wouldn't have meant as much. But from Alli, they meant the world. And all but crumbled his hopes for keeping things strictly businesslike between them.

Alli pulled her Jeep into a parking space outside the supercenter in Brenham Thursday and shifted into Park before eyeing Jake's children in the back seat. Connor was in dire need of some shorts, not to mention T-shirts that covered his entire belly. Not only was the boy growing like a weed, the weather had turned significantly warmer since their trek to the fishing hole Monday evening. And with temperatures forecasted near ninety for Saturday, the boy needed some suitable clothing for the outing with his grandparents.

Jake seemed to have come to terms with his in-laws' impending visit, acknowledging it was the kids they were more interested in spending time with and seemingly looking forward to a few hours of alone time. The idea of clothes shopping with them had him thoroughly intimidated, so Alli had offered to take them instead. That is, after she'd razzed him about it. The guy could tangle with thousand-pound animals all day long, yet shopping for clothes had him tucking his tail and running the other way. Yeah, there was no way she could let that one slip past unnoticed. Not when pushing his buttons had always been one of her favorite pastimes.

Turning off the engine, she reached for the door handle and paused. Only a few weeks ago, she wouldn't have dreamed of teasing Jake ever again. Simply having a conversation with him would've repelled her. And now here she was, not only working for him but reestablishing their friendship and even building on it as they rediscovered something they'd once taken for granted.

Armed with her short list of grocery and other items, she emerged from the vehicle and went to help the kids out of the back seat.

"Can we look at the toys?" Maddy asked as she waited for Alli to unbuckle Connor.

Alli gathered the boy into her arms, then held out a hand to help his sister down. "You have plenty of toys, Miss Maddy. But perhaps we can pick up some bubbles."

"Bubbles?" Shielding her eyes from the sun, she looked up at Alli as she closed the door. "For the bathtub?"

"No, these bubbles are for outside."

The child's curious expression suggested she'd never seen a bubble wand before.

"First things first, though. We need to see about getting you and your brother some clothes."

With Connor perched on her hip and holding Maddy's hand, she continued across the parking lot and into the store.

After settling the children in the shopping cart—Connor in the seat, Maddy in the back—Alli headed in the direction of the children's clothing department, pausing only long enough to grab a bottle of kids' sunscreen she'd spotted at a kiosk in the middle of an aisle.

Sliding plastic hangers along a rack a short time later, Alli said, "Connor, what's your favorite color?"

"Bwoo!"

"I like pink *and* purple."

"Don't worry, Maddy." Alli eyed a pair of elastic waist, cotton blend shorts. "We'll look at the girls' clothing in a bit."

Fifteen minutes and two pouches of fruit snacks later, Alli had a decent stack of shorts and shirts for

Connor, along with a pair of jeans in the next size up from what he was currently wearing, a pair of dinosaur swim trunks and some much-needed socks.

"Alright, Maddy, let's see if we can find anything for you." A process Alli feared would take much longer than it had with Connor. And would likely be more costly if she wasn't careful.

As expected, Jake's little girl was enamored with almost everything pink and/or purple, but they settled on a couple of play dresses, some shorts, a glittery pony shirt and a swimsuit.

"I hungee," Connor said with a sigh as Alli aimed the shopping cart toward the grocery portion of the store.

"Of course you are." The child must be going through a growth spurt, because he'd been eating a lot more this past week. Thankfully, she'd planned ahead.

Bringing the buggy to a stop beside a bin of colorful playballs, she grabbed her purse and pulled out a squeezable yogurt pouch. "Here you go." She looked at Maddy. "Would you like one, too?"

"No, thank you."

"Alli?"

She looked up to find a woman with strawberry blond hair approaching from the opposite direction. She was so thin that her clothes practically hung off of her. And when recognition finally dawned, Alli had to remind herself to breathe.

Tonya Hayes, Lacy's mother, approached Alli's cart, her green eyes dull and underscored by dark circles. "I thought that was you." The woman attempted a smile that failed to reach her eyes.

"Tonya." Her frail appearance had Alli struggling for words. Though she was only in her late twenties, she looked much older. She'd suffered immensely from her addict husband's abuse. Not only the physical wounds he'd inflicted upon her, but the gaping hole left on her heart from the loss of her daughter. If only she would have left him when she'd had the opportunity.

Her gaze darted from Alli to the children, lingering on Maddy, who was about the same age Lacy had been when her short life had been snuffed out. And to Alli's surprise, Tonya smiled in earnest.

Overwhelmed with compassion for the woman, Alli embraced her. Only then did she realize just how thin Tonya really was.

Releasing her, Alli took hold of the other woman's hands. "How are you doing?"

Tonya drew in a shaky breath. "I have good days and bad. But my counselor helps."

"Good. I'm glad you're talking with someone. There are some things we shouldn't keep bottled up inside."

The other woman nodded. "That's what Dr. Milburn said."

Alli released her hands. "What are you doing in Brenham?"

Another weak smile. "I live here now. With my aunt. I needed a change. Austin is too big. And holds too many…" Looking away, she shrugged.

"Memories." Alli finished the sentence for her. "I get it. I recently moved back to the area myself."

Her eyes went wide. "You're not with CPS anymore?"

How could she be, when the fear of losing another child under her watch was too big a burden for her to carry? Though she couldn't tell Tonya that. "I'm hoping to become a teacher. For now, I'm working as a nanny."

Tonya again turned her attention to Maddy and Connor. "They're cute."

"I'm four." Maddy beamed as she held up her fingers.

"You are?" Tonya's eyes seemed to brighten for a moment. "You're almost a big girl."

Maddy nodded emphatically. "Uh-huh. Miss Alli is teaching me to write my letters. Connor just scribbles his, though."

"Maybe you can teach him," Tonya said. "That's what big sisters do."

Finished with his snack, Connor began to whimper.

Alli tried to placate him with a bag of fish crackers, but he wasn't interested. "I'm sorry, but we should get going." Alli checked her watch. "Somebody's nap time is rapidly approaching, and I still have to grab a few groceries."

"I understand." Tonya took a deep breath and met Alli's gaze. "I'm trying really hard. I got a job at a little bookstore downtown and am trying to build a new life. I know Lacy wouldn't want me to give up, so I just keep putting one foot in front of the other for her. No matter how difficult it is."

"Have you thought of getting involved with a church? It's a good way to make friends."

Seemingly embarrassed, Tonya lifted a shoulder. "I haven't been to church since I was a little girl."

"I understand. But you can still talk to God. He's always there. And you can share anything with Him— whatever's on your heart, good or bad, because He already knows everything anyway."

She peered at Alli through a veil of thick, unadorned lashes. "You make it sound so simple."

"That's because it is simple. Jesus said to come to Him for rest."

"Humph. I could use some rest."

Looking at the dark circles under Tonya's eyes, Alli could only imagine how torturous her nights must be.

Nighttime was when those unwanted memories always came calling.

"I'm proud of you, Tonya. I know it's not easy." Alli hugged her again, praying this sweet woman would one day be whole again. "Do you have a phone?"

"Yes."

Pulling her own from the back pocket of her shorts, Alli said, "What's your number?" She punched it into her phone and hit the call button.

When Tonya's phone rang, Alli ended the call. "There. Now you have my number if you ever need to talk."

Another tremulous smile. "Thank you. I really appreciate that, Alli."

Connor grumbled again.

Alli took hold of the cart. "Don't ever hesitate to call me. Anytime."

Tonya's face brightened, and as they went their separate ways, Alli found herself wishing she could do more for Tonya. If Maddy and Connor hadn't been with her, she probably would've taken her by the arm and invited her to lunch. Maybe even tried to locate a church that would take her under their wing, walk with her and guide her toward healing. But taking care of Jake's children was Alli's top priority now. And she wouldn't let her friend down.

Chapter Nine

Jake's Saturday had gotten off to a frenzied start. The owner of the new bull he was planning to pick up on Monday called late Friday night to notify him that he was going to be leaving town Sunday and asked Jake if he could come by and get the Charolais today. Knowing the kids would be with their grandparents, he was fine with that, though it meant he needed to be ready to brand, tag and vaccinate the animal.

So while the kids were still asleep, Jake slipped out to the barn, the app for the video monitors in the kids' room open on his phone so he could keep an eye on them while doing some prep work. Yet while he routinely checked on the kids, he lost track of time. The next thing he knew, it was seven thirty, and the kids were still asleep. Now he'd have to rush to get them fed, dressed and ready before their grandparents arrived.

He was on his way back to the house as Alli drove up. What was she doing there on a Saturday? Not that he minded. He'd take as much time with her as he could get.

His insides turned to Jell-O when she stepped out of her Jeep wearing a pair of cotton gym shorts, an oversize T-shirt and flip-flops with her hair piled atop her head. Even without a trace of makeup, she was gorgeous.

Smiling, she said, "One pony shirt, good as new." She unfurled the purple T-shirt she'd picked up for Maddy the other day. The one his daughter had a melt-down over late yesterday when a portion of the spar-kling pony applique had come unattached at some point during the washing and drying process. So Alli had graciously agreed to take it home and fix it so Maddy could wear it to the wildlife park today.

"You're a lifesaver." Not the first time either. Alli hadn't so much as batted an eye the other day when he'd asked—more like begged—her to take the kids clothes shopping. Though he had felt kind of bad about it after learning she'd run into that poor young mother who'd lost her little girl. Her story was yet another reminder of just how blessed he was to have Maddy and Connor. He couldn't imagine life without either one of them.

Alli arched a brow. "What are you doing out here? I thought you'd be getting the kids ready by now."

"I got tied up in the barn." He explained about the bull.

"You'd better get a move on, then. Need some help?"

He released a sigh. "Would you?"

"So long as you've got coffee."

"Come on, then."

While Jake went to wake up Connor, Alli headed into Maddy's room.

Moments later, he heard his daughter's joyful voice saying, "You fixed it!"

Both kids wanted frozen waffles, so Jake put those in the toaster while Alli scrambled up a couple of eggs. She spooned some alongside the waffles he'd just plated and looked at the kids. "Waffles are yummy, but you need protein, too."

"Your eggs are the bestest," Maddy cheered as she scooped up a forkful.

While Alli stayed with the kids at the table to make sure they ate, Jake poured two cups of coffee. He had just retrieved the creamer from the refrigerator when the dogs barked outside. Glancing toward the front window, he saw his in-laws' vehicle coming up the drive.

"Uh-oh."

"What's wrong?" Alli glanced his way.

He closed the refrigerator. "Guess who's here early?"

Standing, she came alongside him and took the creamer from his hand. "They're probably eager to see the kids." She poured a splash into her cup.

"Yeah, but now I have to spend more time engaging with them."

Swirling a spoon through the steaming liquid, she peered up at him rather matter-of-factly. "You need to put on your big boy britches and learn how to deal, Mr. Walker."

He hated when she was right.

After doctoring his own brew, he put the container back into the fridge before moving to the front door.

He opened it, continuing onto the porch as the couple in their midsixties approached, Beauty and Beast on their heels, looking for attention. "Good morning."

"Morning, Jake." Ted, who always had a ready smile, extended his hand. When Jake took hold, the man whose classic side-part hair now sported more gray than brown, pulled him in for a brief hug. With a slap on the back, he let go.

"I know we're early." Wearing a white cotton blouse over denim capris, Brenda gestured to the white cardboard box in her hands. "But when I recalled those delicious kolaches they make at Plowman's, I decided we should pick up some for breakfast."

"A gal after my own heart." Jake wrapped an arm around the woman with highlighted short brown hair and gave her a gentle squeeze. "Y'all come on in."

"Nana!" Maddy raced toward them as soon as they stepped inside. And when she practically threw herself at Brenda, wrapping her arms around the woman's hips, Jake had to intercept the suddenly precarious box of Czech pastries.

"What am I?" Ted planted his fists on his hips and pretended to frown. "Chopped liver?"

"Pop-Pop!" Connor propelled his little body across the room as fast as his short legs would carry him.

"There's my boy." Lifting him off the ground, Ted tossed him in the air, eliciting a hearty belly laugh from the boy.

Jake continued into the kitchen and placed the box atop the island.

Opposite him, still cradling her coffee cup, Alli nodded toward the living room. "I believe the affection is mutual."

Turning, he took in the heartfelt scene in the living room, a twinge of guilt prodding him. He really should make an effort to either invite the Galloways out or take the kids to see them more often. Sadly, he'd allowed secrets to cause a divide between him and his in-laws. But he was in a no-win situation. If he revealed what Bethany had told him that last day, he might come across as spiteful, and that could widen the chasm between them.

"Come see Miss Alli." Maddy tugged her grandmother's hand.

"Awee." Connor beamed at Ted.

Once again facing the woman in question, Jake couldn't help noticing that Alli had abandoned her coffee and appeared rather self-conscious, tugging on her shirt and brushing the wisps of hair away from her face.

"Ted," Jake began, "Brenda. I'd like you to meet Alli Krenek, the kids' nanny."

"Hello." Alli smiled, her cheeks suddenly pink. "You'll have to excuse my appearance. I don't usually dress this way. I just stopped by to drop off Maddy's shirt."

"The pony was coming off, but Miss Alli fixed it," said Maddy.

"That was very nice of her." Brenda smiled. "It's a pleasure to meet you, Alli. Won't you join us for a kolache?" She gestured to the box.

After a little coercion, Alli agreed to stay, though not without taking on the role of hostess. She put on a fresh pot of coffee and saw to it everyone's needs were met before joining them at the table.

Maddy told her grandparents about all the fun she and Connor were having with Alli, and how they hardly watched television anymore. Something that was, apparently, a big deal for her.

After swallowing a bite of her peach kolache, Alli reached for her coffee. "I want the kids to experience new things for themselves instead of watching other people do them. So we go exploring, garden and do crafts that allow them to learn while having fun."

"Hear! Hear!" said Ted, lifting his mug.

"I done." Connor waved his sticky hands in the air.

Alli scooted her chair away from the table and slid an arm around the boy's waist, gathering him to her. "Let's wash your hands, then we'll get you dressed so you can go on an adventure with Nana and Pop-Pop."

Jake stood to help her, appreciating the way she'd picked up on Ted and Brenda's grandparent names. "What would you like me to do?"

"Nothing." She smiled up at him with those deep blue eyes. "You go enjoy another kolache." They were his favorite breakfast treat. But given that the Galloways were still at the table, he got the impression Alli was, in effect, reiterating her big boy britches comment from earlier.

Nonetheless, he lifted a brow in a silent plea. "You're sure?"

"Positive."

"I'm done, too!" Beside Brenda, Maddy wiggled in her booster seat, so her grandmother slid the chair away from the table, allowing his daughter to escape.

"I can help Alli get them dressed," she said.

As the women and kids disappeared down the hallway, Ted rested his elbows on the table and clasped his hands. "So how are you doing, Jake? I mean between the kids and running the ranch, your hands are plenty full." He let out a low chuckle. "I'm not sure I'd be able to handle everything as well as you are."

"Only because I've had a lot of help, sir. My mom has gone above and beyond. And with Alli adding more structure to the kids' routine, things are running a little more smoothly."

"The kids really seem to like her."

Jake nodded. "She's been good for them. Even got them learning things they would in preschool." He shook his head. "How she manages to do all that and keep the house clean *and* cook is beyond me."

"I assume you ran a background check before hiring her." Ted's brown eyes remained fixed on Jake, his brow pinched.

"Didn't need to. Alli and I grew up together. Her daddy owns the ranch adjacent to ours." He instinctively nodded in that direction. "She's staying there while she works toward a new career as a teacher. Prior to that, she was with CPS for several years." Great, now he was rambling. Something he found easy to do when Alli was the topic of conversation.

"Coupled with what I've witnessed today, it appears she has a real heart for children. After all, CPS can be a tough gig."

"Yes, sir." And Jake was beyond blessed that she'd agreed to help him. He didn't know what he'd do when she left. Finding someone to care for Maddy and Connor was tough in and of itself. But finding someone of Alli's caliber was going to be almost impossible.

Once the kids were dressed and ready, Alli said her goodbyes. The Galloways took off a short time later, leaving Jake to finish prepping things in the barn before hitching the gooseneck trailer to his truck and heading over to Ross Gimble's place.

By early afternoon, he was rolling back up his own drive with his new bull.

Beauty and Beast darted back and forth as he approached the barn, their tails wagging.

Keeping one eye out for them, he backed the trailer up to the pen where he'd prep the bull before introducing him to the herd.

With the trailer in position, Jake shifted into Park and exited to open the metal gate on the pen. He swung it out and to the right before returning to the cab and easing the trailer just inside the pen's opening.

He killed the engine and returned to the back of the trailer. Inside, tucked safely behind a cross gate, the bull snorted as Jake pulled the pin securing the tailgate and opened it wide before tying it to the gate post on the left side of the pen. Then he returned to the pen gate on the opposite side and eased it against the corner of the trailer so the animal would have nowhere to go but into the pen.

Next, he unlatched the cross gate that had the bull trapped near the front of the trailer and gave it a shove. Now all he had to do was wait.

Leaning against the gate, he watched as massive Charolais took his sweet time.

The bull sniffed and snorted, then nodded his white head before ambling across the metal floor of the trailer and into the pen, just the way Jake had planned.

His phone buzzed on his hip. Retrieving it from its holder with one hand, he looked at the screen, smiling when he saw Alli's name. After seeing her this morning, he wasn't sure he'd hear from her again. Not that he didn't want to.

"Hey, Alli."

"Are you home?"

"Yeah. Just unloaded that bull."

"Would you mind if I dropped by? I've got some news I can't wait to share." There was a timidity in her voice that was as unexpected as it was attractive. Coupled with the fact that she wanted to share something with him and, well, he was as tickled as a ten-year-old with a new bike.

"Sure, come on. I'll be in the barn, working this bull."

"Okay. I'll see you in a few."

Ever since that day they picnicked at the swimming hole, their relationship had been progressing. They were definitely growing more comfortable with each other. He liked being with Alli. She knew his flaws and accepted him anyway. However, his yearning for more seemed to grow stronger whenever they were together. But was that because he was lonely, or was it all about Alli? Because even if there was a void in his life, it couldn't be filled by just anyone or anything. So he'd best entrust that yearning to God and see what He had to say.

Re-pocketing his phone, Jake couldn't help wondering what Alli wanted to tell him. He'd heard the smile in her voice, so it must be something good.

Maybe she found a teaching job.

The thought had him cringing. She'd mentioned in passing once that sometimes they made special provisions for new hires who hadn't completed their certification. If that was the case, he'd be back to square one with the whole nanny situation. And just when things were going so well.

His gut tightened. The only thing worse than losing the kids' nanny was that it also meant Alli would likely be leaving Hope Crossing.

Sucking in a breath, he returned his attention to the bull to discover Beast investigating the creature.

"Beast, you'd best watch out. You're not a cat. You've only got one life to live, and tangling with a bull isn't the recipe for a long one."

The little scoundrel began to bark as he circled the bull one final time. But when he turned and raced toward Jake, the bull startled.

Jake looked down as the white fur ball slipped under the gate and darted between his legs.

"Beast—!"

The gate slammed into the side of Jake's head with a force that had him seeing stars. He stumbled, reaching for one of the metal rungs as the bull banged into it a second time. It swung open, crashing into Jake's chest, knocking him to the ground. His head bounced like a ball and air whooshed from his lungs. With a strength that could only come from God, Jake curled into a ball, right before the bull rushed past him in a blur.

Then everything went dark.

While Alli had been a little apprehensive about meeting Jake's in-laws, she found the Galloways to be very sweet. They obviously loved their grandchildren and Brenda had even thanked Alli for, as she put it, brightening the kids' lives. Though she was quick to add that she was grateful for all Joanna had done, and even admitted she wasn't sure she'd have been able to take on the role Jake's mother had.

After leaving Jake's, Alli returned to her apartment for another online training session before getting ready for the day and treating herself to a trip to the library. Unlike her excursions with Maddy and Connor, this visit was purely for *her* enjoyment. Browsing the rows of books while that familiar library scent wrapped around her like a welcoming hug was more relaxing to her than any spa day. And things only got better after that.

While she was there, the librarian approached her, saying she'd observed Alli during her visits with Maddy and Connor.

The way you connect with the children while you're reading, causing them to engage with the story, is a remarkable gift, the older woman had said, filling Alli with the same kind of warm fuzzies she experienced whenever Maddy and Connor hugged her.

But the librarian didn't stop there. She went on to ask Alli if she'd be interested in reading one Saturday a month for children's story hour. And while Alli was flabbergasted by the offer, the feeling only grew when the woman requested permission to pass Alli's contact information on to the librarian in Brenham.

By the time Alli left the library, she felt as though she were floating on air. The thought of making all those children smile had her own growing so wide her cheeks hurt. Then, as if it was the most natural thing in the world, she'd called Jake.

Yet now, as her Jeep rumbled over the cattleguard at the Walker ranch, she couldn't help wondering why she'd instinctively done that. Less than a month ago, she'd wanted nothing to do with Jake Walker. Now he was the one she couldn't wait to share her good news with?

You're friends. Don't overanalyze it.

She'd do well to take that advice. But she couldn't ignore the fact that their relationship was going through some sort of transformation. In many ways, they still knew each other so well. At the same time, though, they were slowly getting to know the person they'd each become. And Alli was finding Jake the man way too intriguing. Like a fantastically wrapped gift that begged to be unwrapped.

So here she was, rolling up his drive, eager to tell him something she could've just as easily shared over the phone. To make matters worse, it wasn't until after she hung up that she remembered the kids were gone and Jake was all by himself. What if he read something into that?

Cringing, she tightened her grip around the steering wheel as she drew closer to the barn where Jake's truck was parked with a large stock trailer extending from the back of it. While she had yet to spot the man himself, Beauty and Beast rushed toward her vehicle,

barking up a storm, which was rather uncharacteristic
for them. Most times they simply woofed a time or two,
alerting them someone had arrived.

She came to a stop sooner rather than later for fear
she might hit one of them. And when she emerged from
her vehicle seconds later, heat and humidity washed
over her, making her glad she'd opted for shorts today.

Instead of greeting her with their usual plea for a
good petting, both dogs continued to bark. They'd take
a few hurried steps away before stopping and looking
back at her as if to make sure she was following them.
Even the normally docile Beauty seemed agitated.

Despite wearing sunglasses, Alli still lifted a hand
to shield the blazing sun as she scanned the covered
pens at the open end of the barn. The trailer gate stood
wide, yet she didn't see a bull anywhere. No Jake either.

"Jake?" she called as she approached, wondering if
maybe he'd gone to the house for something.

Through it all, the dogs continued to bark. Even
louder, if that was possible. And that had an eerie sen-
sation slithering up her spine. Something wasn't right.

Beauty let out a deep woof, startling Alli. Then the
canine darted around the front of the truck, her coun-
terpart on her heels, Beast's high-pitched, incessant
bark making Alli's ears ring.

Shoving her apprehension aside, Alli followed them.
She rounded the driver's side, watching as her four-
legged friends hurried ahead, their repeated yapping
morphing into pathetic whimpers. Then, beneath Beauty's massive form, Alli saw Jake's unmoving body curled
up on the ground.

Her heart raced and she struggled to take a full
breath, yet somehow managed to propel herself toward

him with the speed of an Olympic runner. What if he was dead? Gone forever? She'd never get to—

No, she wasn't going there.

Dear God, please let Jake be okay.

Reaching his side, she dropped to her knees. "Jake!" Her gaze moved from his head to his feet and back, searching for some sort of clue as to what had happened. Only when she spotted his camo ball cap on the ground next to him did she see the blood oozing from a wound just above the ear on his right side.

She checked for a pulse. *Please, God. Please!*

"Yes! Thank You, Jesus!" She tugged her phone from the back pocket of her shorts. "Jake? If you can hear me, please wake up. I *need* you to wake up."

A slight moan escaped his lips, granting her a morsel of relief. His eyelashes fluttered but his eyes remained closed as she dialed 9-1-1.

After a single ring, a female voice on the other end of the phone line said, "9-1-1, what is your emergency?"

Alli pressed a hand against Jake's shoulder when he rolled onto his back "I have a thirty-five-year-old male found unconscious near his barn. He's bleeding from the side of his head."

She glanced about, looking for any sort of clue as to what might have happened. She looked from the vacant trailer to the empty pen and the tubular metal gate swaying in the breeze, her gut tightening while she struggled to swallow the sudden lump in her throat.

"I think he may have been trampled by a bull." She gave them the address, surprised at how calm her voice sounded when her insides were in a frenzy.

"Alli?" Jake squinted up at her. His face was so pale. Though she was encouraged by the fact that he recognized her.

"Don't move, Jake."

"Why?" He shifted slightly. Moaned. "Ow! Never mind."

"EMTs are on their way, ma'am," said the voice on the other end of the phone.

"Thank you." Ending the call, she dropped her phone beside her. Gravel dug into her bare knees as she worked to prevent Jake from moving. "You need to stay still."

With his eyes barely slit, he looked from side to side. "What happened?"

"I think you might have been trampled by that new bull of yours."

Touching a hand to the side of his head, he winced. Then he tried to sit up.

"Be still, Jake. *Please!*" Eyeing her phone, she commanded her voice assist, "Call Daddy on speaker."

Moments later, "What's up, Alli girl?"

"I found Jake unconscious near his barn. I think he may have been run over by a bull. I've called 9-1-1, but not Joanna."

"We're on our way." Alli could just imagine her father glancing at Francie across the kitchen table as he spoke the words. And that was exactly what she'd been counting on. That they'd drop whatever they were doing to help her.

Alli knew Joanna would want to be with her son; however, she was also aware that the woman would be beside herself with worry, so Alli didn't want her behind the wheel.

Jake groaned. "This hard ground is uncomfortable. Can I at least sit up?"

"*No!*" Anxiety had the single word coming out harsher than she'd intended. But she wasn't willing to take any risks. "Stay still. I'll be right back." Standing, she looked at the dogs. "You two stay."

Beauty whined, then dropped alongside Jake, her big head coming to rest on his shoulder.

Alli sprinted to her Jeep to retrieve her hoodie from the passenger seat then hurried back. With the aid of the tiny pocketknife her father had given her when she was twelve, she cut off a portion of one sleeve and set it aside, along with the knife. After folding the sweatshirt into a makeshift pillow, she leaned over Jake. "I'm going to lift your head just enough to give you a little cushioning."

Jake nodded.

She cringed at the hissing sound he made when she moved him.

"Sorry." After lowering his head, she gently placed the fabric she'd cut from the sleeve over his wound. When pain carved lines in his forehead, she smoothed a finger over them, all the while struggling to quell the plethora of emotions coursing through her. If anything happened to Jake—

She squeezed her eyes shut, ignoring the sweat dripping from her brow. What was she thinking? Yes, of course she wanted him to be okay, but where had that sudden desperation come from? After all, until a few weeks ago, they hadn't spoken but a few words to each other in more than a decade and a half. So why was she having all these discombobulated emotions now?

Looking at him again, she trailed her fingers down his cheek, allowing her palm to linger on his chin. Because this was Jake. The boy who'd stolen her heart long ago. And the man who was dangerously close to doing it again.

The sound of tires racing up the gravel drive had the dogs barking again. Beast, anyway.

Standing, Alli dragged an arm across her brow and gave herself a stern shake as her father's truck came into view, a cloud of dust in its wake.

And when he brought the vehicle to a stop, she heard sirens in the distance.

The cavalry had arrived. And Alli would do well to stay in the moment instead of allowing her mind to wander places it had no business going.

Chapter Ten

"I'm fine, Ted. Like I said before, it was only a *minor* concussion," Jake told his father-in-law over the phone late Monday morning when the man called to check on him.

"But you're still resting?"

"Yeah." Though being parked in his recliner while another pony show played on the television was about to do him in. He had a ranch to run. He wasn't used to being idle.

Ted chuckled. "It's killing you, isn't it? You're not accustomed to sitting still."

"No, sir, I'm not." He absently rubbed Beast, who was curled up on his lap. Both he and Beauty, who'd made herself at home beside Jake's chair, had become his shadows.

"I understand. But sometimes God has to force us to be still so He can get our attention."

"That whole 'Be still and know' thing, right?"

"Exactly. So often we bound out of bed with our to-do lists at the top of our minds and rush through our day without ever bothering to check in with our Lord and Savior."

Jake was definitely guilty of that. It usually wasn't

until his head hit the pillow at night that he remembered he hadn't spoken to God all day. No wonder he was so messed up.

"Thanks, Ted. You've given me some food for thought. And thanks again for keeping the kids Saturday." It had been well after dark by the time Alli brought him and his mother home from the hospital. And, boy, had Jake been glad to get out of that place. Thankfully, after monitoring him for several hours, they'd allowed him to leave.

"I'm just glad we were there to help. So are some of the other ranchers around there tending to things while you're laid up? I know how tight-knit communities tend to band together when someone is down."

Shoving a hand through his hair, Jake sighed. "Actually, Alli has taken it upon herself to make sure the ranch keeps running smoothly while my mom watches the kids." Which was why they were staring at the TV instead of playing outside. Though he shouldn't be too hard on his mother. She had taken them out to their little swing set for a while earlier, before temperatures started climbing. He'd even sat on the porch to watch, just so he could get some fresh air.

"No kidding." Ted seemed genuinely impressed.

"Since her daddy's a rancher, she insisted on covering the day-to-day tasks." Meaning Jake didn't get to spend near as much time with her as he'd like.

"Which are?"

"Making sure the cattle have water, checking fence lines. Basically keeping an eye out for anything unusual." Her dad and Justin had located the bull that'd tried to do Jake in and tended to it yesterday, so that was one less worry. Still, with a handful of pregnant cows, a couple of which were ready to calve, there was always cause for concern.

"If there's an issue, she can call her dad to help." Jake wasn't particularly fond of the arrangement, though. He didn't like relying on others. Yet ever since Bethany's death, he'd been forced to do just that.

Maybe God really was trying to tell him something.

"It sounds like both the kids and your ranch are in good hands," said Ted. "So you just concentrate on taking care of yourself and remember that God's grace is sufficient. Brenda and I will continue to pray for you. And don't hesitate to give us a shout if you need anything."

"I appreciate that, sir."

"Alright, son, we'll talk to you again soon."

Jake had just set his phone on the arm of the chair when Alli emerged from the laundry room, clad in jeans, a T-shirt and sock feet, indicating she'd left her boots outside. Her chocolate brown hair was gathered into a long ponytail that trailed from the back of her ball cap.

"Alli!" Maddy hopped to her feet and bounded toward the woman, who promptly lifted his daughter off the ground and kissed her cheek before setting her back down.

"How are you, sweet girl?"

His daughter struck a sassy pose with a hand on her hip. "We're watching pony shows. But now that you're back, we should go esploring instead."

Alli laughed. "Maybe we can find some time for *exploring* later this afternoon. Right now, we need to think about lunch and nap time." Her gaze drifted to Jake, and he wondered if she was aware he'd been staring at her.

This was the first he'd seen her since late Saturday.

Sure, she'd called his mother for status updates and to discuss her plans for covering things at the ranch while Jake was out of commission, but for whatever reason, she hadn't stopped in to visit. And he'd be lying if he said he hadn't missed her.

Her determination to help him with the ranch was something he found incredibly attractive. It revealed things she would never say. Like that she cared and didn't want him to worry. Perhaps more as well, though that could just be his own wishful thinking.

"Miss Awee." Connor pushed to his sock feet and started her way, his smile wide. "Owside?"

Kneeling to his level, she reached for his little hand. "Not right now, buddy. But how would you like some of Mrs. Dottie's macaroni and cheese for lunch?" Just one of the many covered dishes folks had been dropping off since early yesterday morning. The refrigerator was so full, all Alli had to do was heat things up.

Jake watched as his son nodded and hugged Alli's neck, feeling a twinge of envy.

His mother gathered her purse. "Alli, I'm going to head out. I'll be back around five, unless you need me earlier." His mother had spent the last two nights here, just in case there were any issues with him or the kids. And he supposed she'd be here again tonight.

"Five should be fine, Joanna. That'll give me time to tackle a few chores before heading back out to give the ranch a final once-over."

"I should be able to tend things tomorrow." Jake felt like a kid caught with his hand in the cookie jar when both women glared at him.

"*No!*" they said in unison.

"I was there when the doctor said three days at the

earliest—" Mom wagged a finger "—so don't you try pulling one over on me, Jakey."

He gripped the arms of the recliner. "Yeah, yeah."

Once Alli had heated up the macaroni and cheese, along with some ham and green beans, Jake joined them at the table. When the meal was finished, he returned to his recliner while Alli took the kids to their rooms. When she reappeared fifteen minutes later with an armload of dirty clothes and towels and news that the kids were asleep, Jake hoped for a little one-on-one time with her.

Instead, she disappeared into the laundry room, leaving Jake to wallow in self-pity. Why did he get the feeling she was avoiding him?

While what happened with the bull Saturday was still a little foggy, he remembered Alli dropping off Maddy's shirt that morning and then staying for breakfast with the Galloways. He recalled loading the bull over at the Gimble place and bringing it home. And though he was having a hard time remembering anything to do with the bull, he knew he'd talked to Alli.

Closing his eyes, he tried to concentrate. She'd called him. Even now, he could hear the smile that'd been in her voice. She'd been happy about something. That's right, she had some news. News she'd wanted to share with him. Though she never got the opportunity to do that.

A sound in the hallway now had him turning his head to find Alli holding a laundry basket of towels while she closed the door behind her. When she continued into the kitchen, he decided to join her.

"You should be resting," she said when she saw him approach.

"I don't think shuffling in here to sit with you could be considered exerting myself."

Folding a bath towel into thirds, she glanced his way as he pulled out a chair and sat down. "How are you feeling? And don't say fine."

He chuckled. "Well, at the moment I'm under the effects of an over-the-counter pain reliever, so I am, for the most part, fine." When she started to say something, he held up a hand. "I still feel a little foggy sometimes, but it's getting better."

She set the folded towel on the table and reached for another. "Good. I'm glad to hear it."

"I'm sorry you were the one who had to find me, Alli. I know how scary that can be. I still remember that time Mazie bucked you off. I thought you were dead."

"I know the feeling."

"You were in worse shape than I am now, though."

"Which was why you did my chores for a month."

"'Cause I blamed myself for what happened." He toyed with the edge of a napkin someone had left on the table. "Back to Saturday. If I recall correctly, you phoned me right before the incident. That's why you came over." He cocked his head and looked at her. "You said you had some news you couldn't wait to share."

Adding the towel to the stack, she waved a hand, pink creeping into her cheeks. "Yeah, that's not important now."

"What do you mean not important? You sounded pretty excited on the phone."

"That doesn't matter now. What matters is that you're okay."

Standing, he moved beside her and took hold of her hand. "It's important to me."

She stilled, her eyes widening as they locked with his.

Then her phone rang, breaking whatever momentary connection they'd had.

Tugging it from her pocket, she eyed the screen. "I need to take this." Then she disappeared into the other room.

Talk about rotten timing. Jake reclaimed his seat at the table and finished folding the towels, mentally scolding whoever was on the other end of that phone call.

When Alli returned a few minutes later, she was smiling. The kind that lit up her entire face.

And he couldn't help smiling back. "Somebody made your day."

"Yeah." Shaking her head, she eased into the chair next to his. "So when I called you Saturday, I'd just come from the Hope Crossing Library. Evidently, the librarian there has been observing me on my visits with Maddy and Connor and asked me if I would be interested in reading for the children's story hour they host one Saturday a month."

"That's great."

Alli nodded. "Then she asked if she could pass my contact info on to the librarian in Brenham." She paused to catch her breath. "That—" she gestured to the phone she still held in her hand "—was the librarian in Brenham. She wants to meet with me to see if I'd be a good fit for the children's story time they host every Tuesday. I'm supposed to fill out a volunteer form online before I meet with her on Thursday." She chewed her bottom lip. "Do you think your mom would mind watching the kids for a couple hours?"

"Hey, if she can't, I will."

"Assuming you're able. I should be able to take the

kids with me to the story hour, though. That is, if they want to come."

"They will." He watched her, marveling at the extraordinary woman his childhood friend had grown into. "I'm excited for you, Alli. Who knows, this could be the beginning of something you never expected. You could be, like, the story princess that travels to schools and libraries across the region, reading to children, showing them how fun reading can be."

One brow lifted. "Princess?"

"Yeah." He nodded. "I started to say the story *lady*, but that doesn't suit you."

"And princess does?"

"Why not? I mean, any princess worth her salt puts others before herself, has a strong sense of character, is intelligent—and of course beautiful."

Alli puffed out a laugh. "You almost had me convinced, Walker. Till you got to that last one."

"What's wrong with beautiful?"

"*This*—" she waved a hand from her head to her knees "—is not beautiful."

He couldn't help scowling. "Says who?"

"Says me!"

He shrugged. "You're wrong, then."

"Or maybe you need to get your eyes checked." Standing, she continued, "I need to finish up this laundry while the kids are still asleep, so I can take them out for some exploring once they wake up."

"Hey." Catching her by the arm, he stood. "In all seriousness, congratulations, Alli. You have a gift that should be shared. I have no doubt Brenham will want you."

"Thank you." She peered up at him with a sudden shyness that nearly undid him. "You know, I've been so worried about you that I kind of forgot about this whole turn of events until that call. You're the first person I've told."

"I'm honored you shared it with me." He couldn't seem to stop smiling. And as she walked away, he found himself wishing he could be that person she couldn't wait to share everything with. The way things used to be. Before he broke her heart.

"Alli, my colleague in Hope Crossing couldn't say enough nice things about you." Glenda Donahue, a woman in her early fifties with short brown hair and a ready smile, sat behind her desk inside a small office at the Brenham library shortly after three Thursday afternoon. "She was quite impressed with the way you captured the children's attention instead of simply reading to them." Cocking her head, she added, "How do you do that?"

Alli drew in a deep breath, trying to quell a sudden case of the nerves. "That was very kind of her. Despite my own love for the written word, reading it aloud is a skill I've had to hone." Perched on the edge of her seat, she continued. "Several years ago, I began reading to kids at a women's shelter in Austin, and at first it was just me reading to them while they stared at me blankly with their sad little eyes. In my longing to see them smile, I remembered how my mama used to tell me stories when I was little. The way she would draw me in until I felt like I was part of the story.

"I wanted that for those kids. To create a momentary escape. So I started using silly voices, I exaggerated my expressions, asked questions. The next thing I knew, they were smiling. There was a sparkle in their eyes that hadn't been there before." She shrugged. "And that's been my goal and approach ever since."

Leaning back in her office chair, elbows resting on the padded arms, hands clasped in front of her, Glenda smiled. "Alli, you are a breath of fresh air. The world could use more people like you. Those whose goal is to make children smile."

Heat suffused Alli's cheeks. "Thank you, but I don't deserve any credit. It's simply God working through me."

One dark brow lifted. "Yes, but you've allowed Him to do so." Glenda straightened. "Alli, you are *precisely* the kind of person I want for our children's story hour. Do you have any questions?"

Alli could hardly believe it. Barely ten minutes had passed since Glenda greeted her and they were already done. "Just one. I nanny for two adorable children. Would it be alright to bring them with me?"

"Of course. Anything else?"

After a moment, Alli slowly shook her head. "Not that I can think of."

"In that case, how would you feel about starting this coming Tuesday? Story time is at ten thirty."

"I—I'd love to."

Glenda stood and rounded the desk before offering Alli her hand. "Then we will see you Tuesday morning."

Alli shook the other woman's hand, excitement zipping through her. "Thank you so much."

She couldn't seem to stop smiling as she exited the office and made her way across the carpeted floor, passing multiple bookshelves on her way to the exit. She couldn't wait to tell Jake.

Approaching the double doors, Alli did a double

take when she saw the woman who had just entered. "Tonya?"

Lacy's mother turned and smiled, looking far better than she had that day Alli had run into her at the super-center. The dark circles had faded, and her green eyes were brighter. "Hi, Alli."

They hugged briefly.

"You look great," said Alli.

"Thank you. I started a new job at one of the home improvement centers here in town."

"That's awesome. Are you liking it?"

The other woman nodded. "Better pay. Flexible hours. I'm hoping to get my own apartment." She cocked her head. "What are you doing here? I thought you had to be a resident of the town to use the library."

"I had a meeting with the librarian. I'm going to be reading for the children's story hour they have every Tuesday."

Tonya looked confused. "You're not a nanny any-more?"

"I am. Their grandmother agreed to watch them long enough for me to run over here. I'll bring them for story hour, though." Alli's phone buzzed. She pulled it from her pocket and looked at the screen to see Jake's brief text.

How'd it go?

Ignoring the unexpected thrill that danced up her spine, she addressed Lacy's mother. "Speaking of Maddy and Connor, I need to get back to them." Jo-anna was supposed to meet with her traveling compan-ion at six, so Alli wanted to be back in plenty of time. "It was good to see you again."

"You, too." Tonya smiled as she walked away, and that pleased Alli more than words could express.

Outside, there wasn't a cloud in the sky as Alli made her way across the parking lot, and the temperature was near perfect when she hopped in her Jeep. She started the engine before returning Jake's text.

Nailed it! About to head your way.

A second later, a thumbs-up emoji appeared on the screen.

She dropped the phone into one of the cup holders, smiling from ear to ear as she exited the parking lot. And only in part because of her meeting. The rest was due to Jake Walker.

After realizing on Saturday just how strong her feelings for him had grown, she'd tried to create some separation by having Joanna watch the kids while Alli tended the ranch. But the way Jake had celebrated her after Monday's phone call with the librarian and built her up to be some story princess broached every single one of her defenses.

Her only saving grace had been the other things that required her attention. Who would've thought she'd ever be grateful for laundry? But it had provided the escape she needed. Otherwise, she might have done something outlandish, like kiss him. For a man recovering from an injury, he'd looked and smelled way too good.

Since then, it had become increasingly difficult to keep her feelings for Jake in check. Though she desperately wanted things to remain strictly business, that was hard when two people knew each as well as they did. Especially when her traitorous heart had her mind veering off into the land of what-ifs. She couldn't afford what-ifs. Not when she had no intention of staying in Hope Crossing. By this time next year, Lord willing, she'd be somewhere else, starting a new life, teaching children they can do anything they set their minds to.

Besides, those what-ifs had cost her her best friend once before. She didn't want to lose that connection again.

But can you be content being just friends?

Yes.

Maybe.

Her grip tightening on the steering wheel as she maneuvered onto the farm to market road, she let out a groan. For someone who thought of herself as a strong woman, she was a pathetic weakling when it came to Jake.

She turned on the Christian radio station, her heart lightening as she sang along the rest of the way back to the Walker ranch.

Bumping up the drive, she noted that Joanna's vehicle was gone, and Jake was watching the kids play on the playset they were rapidly outgrowing. She really should talk to him about upgrading to something more age appropriate.

Beauty and Beast barked once, their tails wagging at a frenzied pace, then moved to greet her as she rolled to a stop.

She turned off the engine before stepping onto the gravel and gave both canines a quick rub. Straightening, she glimpsed Jake standing on the other side of the hood, and the smile he gave her was nothing short of heart-stopping.

"Can we get the stuff now, Daddy?" Maddy peered up at him.

He chuckled and shook his cowboy-hat-covered head. "Go ahead."

"Yay!" Maddy scurried onto the porch with her brother trailing.

"I hewp." As usual, Connor replaced the *L* with a *W*.

Alli moved to the front of her Jeep. "What's that all about?"

Something mischievous glinted in Jake's gray eyes, making them look more silver. "You'll find out."

A cardinal's song had her peering into the oak overhead.

"Where's your mom?"

"I had to come in for something, so I told her to go on."

Lowering her gaze, Alli saw Maddy hand something to her brother before taking hold of the handle on a brown paper sack and descending the porch.

Jake watched them approach. "Alright, gang, what do we want to say to Miss Alli?"

All eyes moved to her.

"Congratulations!" the three said in unison.

Connor stepped toward her, his arms outstretched as he handed her a cellophane-wrapped bouquet of mixed flowers. "Fwowers." His grin was the cutest.

Kneeling, she gave him a one-arm squeeze. "Thank you, Connor." She breathed in the fragrance. "This was very thoughtful of you."

He tittered as his sister joined them.

Maddy looked every bit as excited as her brother as she held out the bag. "Open it."

"Open it, *please*." Arms crossed over his chest, his biceps bulging, Jake leaned his backside against the Jeep.

Standing, Alli set the flowers on the hood, then

pulled sheet after sheet of tissue paper from the bag. "What's in here?"

"It's a surprise." Hands clasped under her chin, Maddy bounced up and down, reminding Alli of a soda bottle about to spew.

When the paper had all been removed, Alli reached in and pulled out not one, but a stack of four quart-sized galvanized buckets. Her gaze darted to Jake, one brow arching in question.

He lowered his arms and sent her the kind of smile that rendered her defenseless. "Some of the mulberries are ripe. Thought we'd celebrate your new position at the library by doing a little picking. I've got sandwiches and chips for supper and a cooler with a half-gallon of pralines and cream. What do you say?"

The same giddiness that once had her agreeing to a date with Jake welled inside her again. And she was no better prepared now than she'd been back then.

"But it's been less than a week since your accident. Are you sure *you're* up to such an outing?"

"I feel fine. No headaches for two days now. Besides, holding the ladder shouldn't be too taxing."

She felt her smile grow even wider. "In that case, let's go."

Chapter Eleven

Pure joy.

Jake had almost forgotten what it felt like. Holding his children in his arms for the first time. Seeing the love in Bethany's eyes as she walked down the aisle on her father's arm. Those moments when Jake's heart was so full he thought it might explode.

He'd feared they were gone forever. Yet as he reveled in the simplicity of eating ham sandwiches and picking mulberries with purple-stained fingers under a cloudless sky in one of the prettiest spots on God's green earth while the giggles of his children carried on the breeze, something loosened inside him. Pure and unbridled.

Man, did it feel good.

And to think, he'd only wanted to do something nice for Alli. After all she'd done for him and his children, the least he could do was celebrate with her. And the smile that spread across her face from the moment he mentioned picking mulberries until they returned with two buckets full and had them washed, dried and in the refrigerator told him he'd achieved just that.

Now as he roamed the ranch in the utility vehicle the

next day, taking things slow so he wouldn't bounce too much, he paused to observe a cow with her brand-new calf. From the looks of things, his fears that the mama might struggle with her first birth had been unfounded. Both she and her baby appeared to be doing just fine.

He was eyeing his watch, noting it was almost lunch-time, when his phone rang. Pulling it from his shirt pocket, he saw Alli's name on the screen.

"Hey, how's it going?"

"Good. Just letting you know Ted is here, and he'd like to see you."

"Ted? As in my father-in-law?"

"Yes. So why don't you head on back and I'll see if he'd like to join us for lunch." She ended the call before he could respond.

Once again, that heaviness Jake always felt around his in-laws settled into his chest, displacing last night's momentary delight. Why was Ted here anyway? And why hadn't he called first? Jake didn't like being caught off guard. But then, he didn't have any reason to be sus-picious of his father-in-law either.

With Alli's insistence that he learn to deal coming to mind, he sucked in a breath and aimed for the house.

Once there, he found everyone in the kitchen. Ted sat at the table with Maddy and Connor while Alli stood at the counter, stirring mayonnaise into a bowl of chicken. She was good about using whatever leftovers were in the refrigerator. Something he was certain she had learned from Mrs. Angie.

Ted stood when he spotted Jake. "Good to see you on your feet again, son." His gaze roamed from head to toe. "I wanted to see for myself how you were doing. Hope you're takin' things nice and easy."

"Yes, sir. My mama would have my hide if I didn't."

The older man chuckled. "Can't say as I blame her. You gave us all quite a scare." His gaze drifted to Alli. "'Specially that young lady over there."

"I think he shaved a couple years off my life expectancy." She moved to the sink to rinse her hands. "Lunch is about ready."

The kids talked their grandfather's ear off while they ate, allowing Jake to enjoy his chicken salad in relative peace. But once the meal was over and Alli went to put the kids down for their naps, leaving Jake and Ted alone, Jake found himself longing for even a morsel of that joy he'd felt last night.

"Mind if we take a walk?" Ted paused. "That is, if you're up to it."

"Yeah, I'm good." Physically, anyway. He had a feeling there was more to Ted's visit than simply checking on Jake's health. And Jake suspected it had to do with the kids. Specifically, who would care for them if something happened to him. It was something he'd thought about a lot this week. Because while he'd had a will drawn up after Bethany died, naming his mother as guardian of the children, he now wondered if that was the right move. Was it best for Maddy and Connor?

The afternoon air was typical for early May. Warm, but not oppressive. Lord willing, that kind of heat would hold off until July or August.

They strolled beyond the barn, pausing at the fence to survey the cattle-dotted pasture.

"Jake, there's something I need to talk to you about. Something that's been weighing on me since Bethany's death."

Jake groaned inwardly. This was about the kids, alright.

"At first, it didn't make sense to say anything because she was gone. But lately I've been feeling like I need to share something with you. Even more so since meeting Alli."

Shoving his hands in his pockets, Jake lifted a brow. "What does Alli have to do with anything?"

His father-in-law peered up at him. "Perhaps nothing. On the other hand, it could also impact both of your lives."

Now Jake was genuinely confused. "Care to explain that?"

"I realize you and Alli have been friends for a very long time. However, both Brenda and I witnessed something more between the two of you. Something I don't think either of you realize. Or are simply doing your best to ignore." The man rocked back on his heels. "Having been a pastor for a long time, I've counseled folks with a lot of different issues. And one thing I've witnessed, particularly in younger people like yourself, is that they're afraid to move on after losing a spouse for fear they'll be disrespecting that person."

That wasn't an issue for Jake. "I appreciate what you're doing here, Ted, but—"

The man held up a hand. "Jake, I'm not here to give you permission to move on with your life. I'm here to ease my conscience. And it's difficult because I'm afraid I'll be hurting you in the process."

Jake felt his gaze narrow. While he doubted anything Ted might say could hurt any worse than his daughter's parting words, whatever it was had the man very conflicted. "In that case, go ahead."

A cow bellowed in the distance as Ted struggled for words.

Moments later, the calf echoed its mama.

Finally, "Bethany—" The older man covered a sob.

Jake set a hand on his shoulder and waited, his lunch feeling like a lead weight in his stomach.

Ted cleared his throat and straightened. "About a week before she passed, Brenda and I had gone out to eat one night. We'd decided to try some new restaurant across town instead of one of our usual places. And—" his lips quivered "—Bethany was there."

Jake's muscles tightened.

"Except she wasn't alone." The older man's voice cracked as tears spilled onto his cheeks. "She was with another man, Jake." Again, he cleared his throat, anger darkening his expression. "And it was obvious they were more than friends."

Jake's eyes closed, and while the image that formed in his mind should've enraged him, it didn't. All he could do was shake his head.

He squeezed the older man's shoulder. "It's okay, Ted."

"Okay?" Ted jerked his gaze to Jake's, his face red. "How can you—?"

Jake held up a hand. "Let *me* finish."

The man nodded.

"The night Bethany died, before she left the house, she said she wanted a divorce. She told me she was in love with someone else."

Ted's eyes widened. "Why didn't you tell us?"

"Because it would've hurt you and Brenda, and I couldn't do that, no matter how angry I was. You and Bethany's children deserve to have good memories of her."

"I'm sorry, Jake. That is not how we raised our daughter."

"I know, so don't blame yourself. I've done enough of that for all of us."

"Bethany made her choices. You're not to blame either."

"Oh, I'm not so sure about that." Hands now in his pockets, he stared off in the distance, welcoming the breeze that swept across the vibrant pasture. "Bethany didn't have any friends out here. I was trying to keep up with the ranch the way my dad always had, so she was alone a lot."

"But she had the kids. And it's not like you were neglectful."

"You say that—" he regarded the man "—yet I never noticed she was unhappy either. At least, not until it was too late."

The man clapped a hand against Jake's back. "None of us is without sin, Jake. The important thing is that we learn from our mistakes. You're a good man."

"More like a work in progress."

"We all are." He paused. "I believe Alli has been good for both you and the children."

"I couldn't ask for a better nanny. But she's only temporary. Once she's set to move into teaching, she'll be leaving." And finding someone who came even remotely close to filling her shoes wasn't going to be easy. Because once again, he'd be losing his best friend.

"Wasn't that a silly mouse?" Alli closed the cover on her last book at the Brenham library Tuesday morning, her heart full as she scanned the dozen-plus smiling faces before her. "How many of you like milk with your cookies?" Still perched on the kid-sized chair, she raised her hand, as did each of the children sitting cross-legged on the floor, including Maddy and Connor.

Unable to stop smiling, she said, "Thank you for being such good listeners today. Did you have fun?"

To her delight, the response was a resounding "Yes," or some variation thereof.

"That's all the time we have for today, but I hope you'll come back and let me read to you again sometime."

As parents collected their children, a woman close to Alli's age approached with two little girls who looked to be about two and four.

"My girls have always enjoyed coming for story time, but you have taken it to a whole different level. Between your expressions and the voices, *I* couldn't wait to see what was going to happen next."

Motioning for Maddy and Connor to join her, Alli chuckled. "I appreciate the encouragement. Sometimes it's a fine line between capturing their attention and pure ridiculousness."

"Well, this was amazing. We will definitely be back next week."

"In that case, I hope to see you then."

As the mom departed, Maddy slumped against Alli's leg. "I'm hungry."

"Me, too." Connor tilted his head all the way back and stared up at her.

"Well—" she stooped to their level "—since you two were so very good today, perhaps we can pick up some lunch on our way home."

Their eyes lit up.

"Let me gather my things." Standing, she saw Tonya coming toward them.

While there was some slight shadowing beneath her eyes, she still looked good overall. More importantly, she was smiling. "I saw that today was the story time, so I thought I'd stop by. You're very good."

"Thank you. It was fun."

"I remember you from the store." Maddy smiled up at Tonya.

"I remember you, too." Her face brightened as she stooped to Maddy's level. "I'm Miss Tonya."

"I'm Maddy." She poked a thumb to her chest before pointing to her brother. "He's Connor."

Suddenly shy, he looked up at Alli. "I hungee."

She smoothed a hand over his white-blond hair. "You are a bottomless pit, little one." Turning her attention to Tonya, she said, "Thank you for coming by to support me. I really appreciate it."

"It was fun. Maybe I'll drop by again sometime."

"I'd like that." It did Alli's heart good to see Tonya moving on with her life.

After gathering her things, Alli escorted the kids to the parking lot where she buckled them into her Jeep before heading to the drive-in burger joint. And as soon as the kids were settled with their chicken tenders, she continued on to Hope Crossing, noshing on Tater Tots while kids' music spilled through the speakers. Until her phone rang, anyway.

She glimpsed the dashboard to see Tori Stallings's name. "Sorry, kids. I have to interrupt your music." After pressing the hands-free icon, she said, "Hi, Tori."

"Alli. How are you?"

"Doing well. Yourself?"

"Ready for school to be out. The kids are always restless this time of year." She paused. "Hey, I'm calling because I have something I'd like to discuss with you. Would you be available to meet one night this week?"

Alli couldn't imagine what Tori might want with her. She'd heard they were needing more volunteers for Bible school next month. Maybe that was it. But couldn't they just discuss that over the phone? Unless

Tori had gotten wind of a teacher opening. Not that Alli had ever contemplated staying in Hope Crossing. But then, when she came back home, she never imagined she'd be spending her days at Jake's house, caring for his children. Or that her feelings for him would be precariously teetering a fine line between friendship and something more.

But then, that didn't mean Jake shared those same feelings. Even if he had taken the time and effort to plan an endearingly fun evening of berry picking last week.

"Sure. I can do tonight, if that works for you. I know you've got Aiden to consider, though."

"His grandmother has already said he can stay with her, so why don't I come by your place?"

"Sounds good. Is six thirty okay?"

"Perfect."

"Just come up the stairs along the side of the garage."

"Got it."

"I don't suppose you can give me a hint as to what this is about."

"I could, but it would only lead to more questions, so I'd prefer to wait."

"Okay, now you've really got me curious."

Her friend chuckled. "I promise I'll explain everything tonight."

Alli's mind raced the rest of the way back to Jake's. But once she arrived, it was work as usual. To her surprise, the kids went down for their naps without protest. While they slept, she called Jake to let him know she'd need to leave early, then assembled a casserole for supper, and when the kids woke up, the three of them weeded and watered their garden. They already had some cucumbers and tomatoes on the vine, though they were still in their infancy.

Alli was pushing Connor on the too-small swing while Maddy rolled around the grass with Beast, Beauty supervising the lot of them, when Jake's truck came rolling up the drive, towing a utility trailer. And when he parked and got out, he was all smiles.

Moving out from under the shade of the oak tree, Alli noticed multiple cardboard boxes on the trailer, one of which was very large. "Whatcha got there?"

"Something you've been telling me the kids are in desperate need of."

When she saw him eye the playset behind her, her jaw dropped. "No way." Had he really broken down and bought them a new swing set?

"You're right." Hands slung low on his hips, he shrugged. "It's time for something bigger."

It took everything inside her not to hug him.

"Gotta get it built first, though. Too bad you're planning to run off."

Now she wished she'd selected another day to meet Tori. "I can help you tomorrow."

"Help with what?" Maddy looked from Alli to Jake.

"Just some project your daddy's working on." She eyed her watch. Five thirty. "I'm going to get supper on the table and then I need to go."

"Still no guess as to what Tori wants to discuss with you?"

"Nope. Unless it's a job opportunity." She shrugged.

When she finally made it back to her place, she had just enough time to scarf down some of the casserole she'd brought from Jake's and change into a comfy T-shirt dress before Tori knocked on her door.

"Oh, my." Tori's blue eyes were wide as she entered the tiny apartment. "This place is adorable. It looks like it came straight out of a magazine."

"Doesn't it, though? Francie did a really nice job."

Looking at Alli, Tori said, "I need to hire her to help me with my house."

"I'm sure she'd love to." Alli closed the door. "So, your rather cryptic phone call has had my curiosity piqued all day." She motioned to one of the lounge chairs.

Dressed in denim shorts and a pink T-shirt, Tori sat down as Alli perched on the chair opposite. "Sorry about that. It was my lunch period, and I was afraid if I got started explaining I'd be late getting back to class."

"Whatever it is, you seemed very excited."

Her friend laughed. "That's because I am." She clasped her hands in her lap. "So Midge Cahill, who owns the day care in town, is planning to retire this fall. And since no one expressed an interest in taking it over, she was going to close the day care altogether."

"Oh, no. That would impact a lot of people."

"I know. I'm one of them." Tori shook her head. "Not to mention many of my colleagues. I even contemplated buying it myself. But aside from the fact that I can't afford it, between teaching and being a single mother, there's no way I could pull it off. So I had to come up with another option."

Surely Tori didn't want Alli to buy the place. "Which is?"

"After talking with my principal, we approached the district superintendent, who contacted Midge about the possibility of leasing the facility. When she agreed, he contacted the Texas Workforce Commission regarding start-up funding for a district-run early learning center. And last week, the school board voted in favor of the project. The school district will cover the center's day-to-day operations and district employees will staff it. In addition, it will provide an education training pathway for high school students wanting to explore different career fields."

"And what would they do?"

"Whatever the teacher feels they can handle. Some might act as more of an aid while upper-level students could plan and present lessons. Under a teacher's observation, of course."

"That sounds like a really good idea, Tori. But I'm not sure why you're telling me about it. Unless this is your way of letting me know there will be some teaching positions opening up soon."

"While that is most definitely a possibility, I would prefer to see you in the role of director."

Alli felt her eyes widen. "Director? Me?"

Tori nodded. "First of all—" she held up a finger "—you've said you were interested in preschool or early elementary." She raised a second finger. "And you were with CPS, so you're familiar with the ins and outs of the system. We have at least one foster family in the area and, as you know, foster children can only attend approved centers in order for the state to cover the cost."

"But I'm barely into my courses and haven't had any observation time."

Clasping her hands in her lap, Tori smiled. "You can be granted an emergency permit that's good for a year. As long as there is at least one certified teacher on staff—which there would be—you can serve as director while completing the required training for your certification. Which, in my book," she said with a shrug, "makes this a win-win situation." She cocked her head. "That is, assuming you're interested."

"I—I don't know. I mean, what makes you think I'd be qualified?"

"Alli, formalities aside, you have one of the biggest

hearts for children I've ever seen. That puts you at the top of my list. Do you know how many teachers would love to have your ability to connect with children the way you do?"

Blowing out a breath, Alli leaned back in her chair, gripping both its arms. "I don't know, Tori. Teaching is one thing, but running an entire school? Not to mention the fact that staying in Hope Crossing was never my plan."

"Because you had a job that required you to live in Austin. Now you're free to go wherever you want."

Alli shook her head in disbelief. "I don't know, Tori."

"Will you at least think about it?"

"Yes, I'll definitely do that." Once she wrapped her brain around the idea and did a little research.

"Good." Tori shot to her feet like the bouncy little cheerleader she'd been back in high school. "If you have any questions, don't hesitate to contact me."

"Trust me. I won't."

Tori hugged her before leaving Alli with a whole lot to consider. Was she as capable as Tori believed her to be? Being near her father would be nice. Though staying in Hope Crossing would mean watching Jake, Maddy and Connor go on without her in their lives. And as much as she hated to admit it, that was something that would be much easier to do from afar.

Chapter Twelve

There were some things only God could do. Such as creating a brand-new job opportunity right here in Hope Crossing that had Alli's name written all over it. If only Alli would see it that way.

The sun shone bright the next morning as Jake unpacked the wood pieces, hardware and accessories that would make up the kids' new swing set. Alli had called him last night after Tori left her, wound up tighter than a top. How a person could be so excited yet skeptical and uncertain at the same time was beyond him. *You know what they say, Jake. If it's too good to be true, it probably is.*

Or it could be God's provision, he'd responded. Even if it meant he'd lose the best nanny he and the kids could've asked for, it would be worth it if Alli stayed in Hope Crossing where he could see her every day, maybe even take her on that long-overdue date he couldn't seem to stop thinking about. And while he knew better than to get his hopes up, he was going to do his best to convince her this new position was perfect for her.

Alli and the kids appeared on the porch as the sound of tires on gravel had him turning to see his mother's vehicle coming up the drive. She'd agreed to keep an eye on the kids while he and Alli worked to build the swing set. Even though the holes had been predrilled, he suspected it would take them the better part of the day to assemble the thing.

"What are you doing, Daddy?" Maddy eyed the pieces sprawled across the grass. "What's all this stuff for?"

Alli looked his way, her brow lifted in question.

"What do you think? Should I tell them?"

"Why not?"

"In that case…" He retrieved the now-empty box with the image on it. "While you and Connor play with Mimi today, Miss Alli and I are going to be building *this* for you guys."

His daughter's eyes went wide, and her mouth dropped open when he turned the picture so she could see it. "A big kid swing set!" She rushed toward him and threw her arms around his legs. "I can't wait to play on it."

Smoothing a hand over her soft curls as she smiled up at him, he said, "You'll have to be patient. It's going to take us a while to get it built."

"Like, after my show?"

He shook his head. "Like, maybe by suppertime."

"Aw." Her shoulders slumped and her head drooped. "That's *so* long."

"Sorry, Madikins." He cupped her chin. "But once it's finished, you can play on it as long as you like."

"Forever?"

"Okay, maybe not that long. But how 'bout till bed-time?"

Her face brightened. "And then I can do it again when I wake up tomorrow."

His mother closed her car door and headed toward them. "What's going on?"

"Daddy and Miss Alli are building me and Connor a new swing set."

"How exciting!"

"Can we stay out here and watch them?" Maddy pleaded.

"Hmm." His mother touched a finger to her chin. "We could. Or, since it's nice and warm today—" setting her hands on her knees, she stooped to Maddy's level "—we could go to the park in Brenham and play in the water at the splash pad."

Maddy's gasp was audible. "I want to go to the splash pad!"

"I go, too." Connor wiggled toward his grandmother, who promptly picked him up.

The splash pad? Jake assumed she'd just watch the kids here. "Are you sure? I mean, that place can get kind of busy." What if she lost track of one of the kids?

"Not when school is still in session." Setting Connor back on the ground, Mom waved Jake off. "We'll be fine. Besides, my friend Ginny is going to meet us so we can discuss our trip."

Since Alli had taken over sitting for the kids, his mother had either shopped or had supper with her traveling companion at least once a week. What more could they have to discuss? And what if they got so engrossed in conversation they failed to monitor the kids properly?

He felt a sudden jab in his ribs. "Ow." Glancing to his left, he saw Alli glaring up at him.

"Stop worrying," she whispered. "This'll be good for all of them. And they won't be parked in front of the television."

How did she always seem to know what he was thinking? "Good point."

"Come on, my darlings." Mom took hold of their

hands. "We need to get your swimsuits, a change of clothes, towels and some sunscreen. Then we'll stop by Mimi's house and pack a picnic lunch to take."

"The splash pad *and* a picnic!" Maddy beamed. "This is the bestest day *ever*!"

By the time they pulled out of the drive a half hour later, Jake agreed he was probably just overreacting. He was so used to his mother staying here with the kids, it never crossed his mind they would go somewhere. But they'd be fine. Mom would never put Maddy or Connor at risk.

"So where do we start?" Wearing a pair of cutoffs and an A&M T-shirt, her hair in a ponytail, Alli awaited her instructions.

It wasn't until he looked down at her that he realized it would be just the two of them for the next few hours. That brought a smile to his face.

"Why don't you assemble the ladder while I work on the swing beam?" He pointed out the parts for the ladder. "The instructions are on the workbench." He nodded in the direction of the two sawhorses he'd topped with an old sheet of plywood.

"Now I know why you told me to bring Dad's drill." She started toward her Jeep. "I'll be right back."

Soon, they set to work on each of their tasks, the whirr of drills filling the rapidly warming air. He was glad he'd had the forethought to set things up under the old oak where they'd have plenty of shade. Sadly, the constant noise made conversation impossible, and he was dying to know what direction Alli's thoughts on Tori's offer were headed this morning.

So as soon as there was a lull, he asked, "Have you thought any more about your meeting with Tori?"

"Only all night long." She dragged her forearm

across her brow. "I don't suppose you've got any water out here, do you?"

He pointed to the red cooler beneath the table. "In there."

"Oh, good." Lifting the lid, she grabbed a sweaty bottle before continuing. "I'm just afraid it'll be too much for me. I mean, I'm not even a teacher yet."

"I thought Tori said that wasn't a problem."

Her shoulders sagged. "She did. But what if it turns out to be more than I can handle?"

"Alli, she wouldn't have come to you if she didn't think you were qualified." He grabbed his own water bottle and twisted off the cap. "Seems like the only one doubting you is you."

"It's more than just that, though."

"Like what?"

"I already had a plan, and it didn't involve staying in Hope Crossing."

"Are you saying you don't want to stay here?"

Her gaze drifted to the pasture. "I've never considered it before."

"Perhaps you should."

"I don't even know what a life here would look like." She took another swig. "Living in a garage apartment at my dad's is fine for the short term, but I need my own space."

"So you find a house."

"Like there are so many available in Hope Crossing."

"It only takes one. Have you ever even checked?"

"No." She had yet to look at him. Instead, she toed at a clump of grass. "I guess I've gotten used to living in the city. All the options there. The convenience of everything." Finally, she met his gaze. "But it feels good to be back home, too."

The fact that she still referred to Hope Crossing as "home" gave him hope. "You've been gone a long time, Alli. Your perspective has changed. *You've* changed. Perhaps you'll find Hope Crossing is where you belong after all."

She absently toyed with her water bottle. "Or prove once and for all that it's not the place for me."

His heart squeezed, but he wasn't about to throw in the towel. She needed to be challenged, just the way they used to do with each other when they were kids. Alli knew what she wanted. She was simply afraid to go after it.

"Then at least you'd know for sure, and you could put the speculation behind you. Which begs an even bigger question."

After a moment, she looked his way. "Which is?"

"Have you got the guts to try?"

The only thing Alli hated worse than being challenged was being challenged by Jake.

She looked up at the graying clouds stretched across the northwestern sky late the following Monday afternoon and pushed the kids on their new swing set while the dogs looked on, still wrestling with Jake's comments about staying in Hope Crossing. How was it possible that after all these years he still knew her so well? And could she say the same about him?

Without a doubt. She'd been reading him like a favorite book since she arrived. Like when he'd dismissed her offer to nanny the children—she'd known he would change his mind.

"I wanna play on the fort." Maddy dragged her feet along the ground, slowing her movement before hopping out of the belt swing and scurrying to the short ladder.

"I pway fowt, too." Connor wiggled inside his bucket swing.

"Hold on, buddy." Gripping the plastic-covered chains on each side, she eased him to a stop before lifting him to the ground and following him toward his sister. "Careful on the ladder." She stood beside him until he was safely in the fort.

Crossing her arms, she watched the kids draw on the chalkboard affixed to the wall of the fort. For as much as it irked her, she couldn't deny that sense of comfort in the familiarity between her and Jake. And that left her with feelings that were exhilarating and petrifying at the same time. And sure as the sunrise every morning. She knew it just as well now as she had when she was seventeen.

Sadly, no other man had affected her that way since. Not even the one she'd planned to marry.

"Miss Alli! Watch!" All smiles, Maddy sat down on her bottom at the top of the slide.

Alli couldn't help but smile back. "I'm watching."

When the girl reached the bottom, Connor was working himself into position. "Watch me Miss Awee."

She did as he, too, zoomed down the plastic slide. Then scooped him into her arms when he reached the bottom.

"Again, again," he giggled.

Supervising another trek up the ladder, Alli thought back to that day Jake had asked her to go to the movie with him. Her hopes had been so high, only to be squashed. Looking back, she regretted not allowing him to apologize. Who knows what might've happened then?

But fear had kept her from following her heart. And here she was, seemingly destined to let that happen again. To what end, though? A life bogged down in what-ifs and might-have-beens?

Perhaps it was time for her to act like the bold woman people thought her to be. Not that she'd ever been good at acting. What if Jake wasn't interested in anything more than friendship?

Thunder rolled across the darkening sky, causing Beast to whine while Beauty stood, nose in the air.

"Okay, you two," Alli said to the kids. "That's our signal to go inside."

"But we're having so much fun," Maddy whined from the top of the slide.

"We'll play tomorrow. Right now we need to get inside where we'll be safe from the storm."

A loud clap of thunder punctuated her statement and had Maddy zipping down the slide while poor Connor stood at the top, looking panic-stricken.

Alli gathered him into her arms and started toward the house as the wind picked up.

"I don't like storms." Maddy frowned as they stepped inside.

Standing Connor on the floor in the laundry room, Alli said, "I know they sound kind of grumbly, but they also bring rain to water our garden and give the plants important nutrients that help them grow."

Maddy cocked her little head. "What are nutrents?"

"Nutrients," Alli gently corrected. "Like what's in your gummy vitamins."

Maddy rubbed her tummy. "Mmm, I like gummy vitamins."

"I, too." Connor mimicked his sister.

A loud crack of thunder rattled the house.

The children latched on to her, whimpering.

Their actions reminded Alli of a children's book enti-

tled *Thunder Cake* she'd read at the shelter a while back.
A story about a little girl who was terrified of storms,
until her grandmother distracted her by gathering the
ingredients and then baking their Thunder Cake to eat
at the height of the storm.

A cake might be a bit of a stretch for these two, but
perhaps Alli could use the same technique to distract
them. She quickly pondered what all was in the house.
"Who wants to make some Thunder Crisps?"

"What are Thunder Crisps?" Maddy's little face contorted in a curious expression.

"They are yummy treats we can only make when
it's thundering."

"What kind of treats?" The girl's eyes were wide.

"They have crispy rice cereal, butter and *marshmallows*."

Maddy bounced. "I like marshmallows."

"I, too." Connor wiggled.

"Okay, let's gather our ingredients."

Thunder rumbled again.

"Maddy, would you and Connor please find the cereal and marshmallows in the pantry while I get the
butter?"

"Yes, ma'am."

Once they had their ingredients, Alli placed a chair
on either side of her at the island. One for each child.
Then she added the appropriate amount of butter into a
large bowl before showing Maddy how to measure the
marshmallows. Connor got to dump them into the bowl.

The microwave melted the butter and marshmallows
in no time. Then Maddy measured the crisped rice cereal and Connor dumped it into the bowl. Eyes wide,
the kids watched with rapt attention as Alli stirred everything together.

And all the while, the storm grew closer, yet they didn't seem to notice. Especially after the mixture was in the pan and she offered to let them lick the bowl and spoon once they'd cooled sufficiently.

Rinsing her hands at the sink, Alli peered out the window to discover a sky the color of graphite. Trees were being whipped into a frenzy by the wind.

And Jake was out there somewhere. He'd gone over to Prescott Farms to help Justin with something more than an hour ago.

Her phone buzzed in the back pocket of her shorts, startling her. She hurriedly dried her hands before retrieving it. Seeing Jake's name, she tapped the screen and placed the phone to her ear.

"Jake, where are you?"

"There's a twister headed your way." His voice was level and intense. "Take the kids and get into the closet under the stairs. Now!"

Alli felt her eyes widen while panic built inside of her like steam in a kettle. "Where are you?"

"No time—"

"Hello? Jake?"

The line was dead.

She promptly called him back, but it went straight to voice mail.

Lightning flashed outside the window a split second before thunder boomed, shaking the entire house.

The kids cried and rushed to her side.

Rain began to fall, building to a deafening level. Then Alli realized it was hailing.

"Come on." Taking hold of their little hands, she led them into the hallway. "Beauty and Beast, y'all come, too." Across from Maddy's room, she opened the door to the closet where she'd found Joanna's old picnic basket, turned on the light and urged the kids inside the rather musty space.

After making room for Beauty's massive form, Alli closed the door and sat down on the floor to pull the kids into her lap.

"Why are we in here?" Maddy pouted.

"So we'll be safe if the hail breaks any windows." Or a tornado. But she had no desire to explain that.

"It wowd." Connor covered his little ears with his hands.

She pressed his head against her chest. "I know, buddy."

"We should pray," said Maddy.

Out of the mouths of babes.

Alli squeezed her tighter. "That's a very good idea. Let's bow our heads." She sucked in a breath. "Dear God, we know You are with us even in the midst of the storm. We ask that You protect us and that the storm pass quickly." *And please be with Jake. Protect him and bring him home safely.* "We pray this in the mighty name of Jesus, Amen."

As both children pressed into her, she gently stroked their hair with her fingers and continued praying silently for Jake. What if something happened to him? What if he didn't make it home? She thought back to that day she'd found him on the ground, unconscious. The emotions that had risen to the surface. Now here she was again, fighting those same feelings. *God, I don't want to be hurt again.*

She wasn't sure how much time had passed when the sounds from the storm began to diminish, and the kids' little bodies began to relax.

Looking up at the light, she thanked God they still had electricity. That had to be a good sign, right?

"Alli? Maddy! Connor!"

Beast woofed.

Jake?

"Daddy!" Maddy scrambled to her feet.

Alli did, too, taking Connor with her. She pushed open the door, allowing the dogs to escape first. "In here!"

Lines etched his face when he met them in the hallway. "Thank You, Jesus." He lifted Maddy into his arms and kissed her cheek before reaching for his son, who eagerly went to him.

"We hided in the closet," said Maddy.

"That was a very smart thing to do." His gaze drifted to Alli. "My phone died."

Her body relaxed a notch. "I was praying that was the case."

"Daddy, we made Thunder Crisps." Maddy patted his cheek. "Want some?"

"Thunder Crisps?" Again he looked at Alli.

"You know. Those special treats we make when it thunders." She winked.

"Do you think they're ready?" Maddy looked at Alli.

"Yes, I believe they are."

And just like that, Jake's children forgot all about the storm. Life was back to normal as far as they were concerned. But the intensity in Jake's gaze as he settled them at the table with their treats and a tablet playing their favorite pony show told Alli that nothing was normal anymore.

Needing some distance, she made her way back down the hall. She turned off the light in the closet and was closing the door when Jake approached.

"I'm so thankful you're alright. When I saw that funnel cloud headed this way, I was scared." He reached for her hand. "You're shaking."

"I'll be alright."

"Thank you for protecting my children." He entwined his fingers with hers, sending a keen awareness zipping through her.

"I promised you I would."

He took a step closer, cupping her cheek with a calloused hand. One familiar with hard work, yet tender enough to soothe a hurting child.

Goose bumps raised the hairs on her arms as she stared into his eyes, seemingly helpless to look away. And the certainty she saw there encouraged her. Made her believe that, just maybe, they could have the kind of relationship that lasted forever.

She closed her eyes. *God, I don't want to be hurt again.*

Suddenly, Jake's lips covered hers. Soft and warm, just the way she'd always imagined. He smelled of fresh air, hard work and marshmallow.

Too soon, he pulled away.

Opening her eyes, she saw him smiling down at her. A smile unlike any he'd given her before.

She rested her forehead against his chin. "Jake, what are we doing?"

"I'm not certain." He wrapped his arms around her. "But it feels a lot like something that starts with an *L*—" he kissed her temple "—and ends with an *E*."

Shaking her head, she met his gaze. "I can't, Jake."

"Why not?" He kissed the corner of her mouth.

"What about my plans? I'm supposed to be leaving."

He studied her again, his brow puckering. "Does that mean you've dismissed Tori's offer?"

"It wasn't an offer. It was only a suggestion."

"That you have yet to check in to."

She swallowed hard. Oh, how she wanted to stay.

For whatever was happening between her and Jake to be real. But— "This scares me, Jake."

"Me, too. But I'd hate to miss out on what could possibly be the best thing that has ever happened to me." He brushed her hair away from her face. "We can take things slow, Alli. I won't rush you."

"What if they don't work out?"

"What if they do?"

Here she was, in Jake's arms, listening to him say things she'd longed to hear, and all she could say was, "Can I get back to you? I'm just—" She had to force herself to step out of his embrace. "Both of our emotions are running really high right now because of the storm and—"

"You think I'm caught up in the moment. That I'm going to change my mind."

"No…" *Liar.*

"Okay, then you're afraid I *could* change my mind. But I won't, Alli. And just to prove my point—" He kissed her again, with an intensity that hadn't been there before. One that ignited sparks. Maybe even fireworks. And how she longed to believe him.

But she couldn't. Not yet. She needed to sleep on it and come back when her emotions weren't all over the place. Jake, too.

Because he'd changed his mind once before. And if he did that again, their friendship would never recover.

Chapter Thirteen

Alli arrived at Jake's the next morning, feeling more than a little hesitant. After tossing and turning most of the night, she'd finally fallen asleep only to awaken with feelings every bit as intense as they'd been last night. Ones that had her seriously contemplating calling Tori about that director position. Because no matter how long Alli stared at her reflection in the mirror, telling herself she could not have these kinds of feelings for Jake Walker, her heart refused to acquiesce.

Now, as she dodged a puddle on her way to Jake's back porch, she found it difficult to take a deep breath. Anxiety squeezed her chest. Thankfully, this was her day to read at the library in Brenham, so she wouldn't have to make up an excuse to escape.

Jake swung open the door as she approached, Connor in his arms, his little head resting listlessly on his daddy's shoulder, fingers in his mouth. "I'm glad you're here." He smoothed a hand over his son's back. "Little guy here is sick. I was up with him half the night."

"Oh, no." She moved beside him to feel Connor's rosy cheek. "Fever?"

Jake nodded. "He threw up once, too."

She couldn't help pouting. "Poor baby."

Connor lifted his head and looked at her. His blue eyes lacked their usual spark.

"I'm sorry you're sick, Connor."

When he held his little arms out to her, she immediately took him, noting how warm his body felt.

"Have you given him anything for the fever?"

"About thirty minutes ago. Hopefully it'll kick in soon." Holding the door wide, he motioned her inside.

"Any guess as to what's wrong?"

Jake closed the door and let go a sigh as he followed her into the living room. "I'm guessing it's another ear infection. Nothing a round of antibiotics won't take care of."

She eased into the glider and gently moved back and forth. "I guess you'll be taking him to the doctor, then."

"I'll put a call in as soon as they open." Hands on his denim-clad hips, he stared down at her. "And I've already asked Mom to come and stay with him while you're in Brenham."

The fact that he remembered her schedule in the midst of a crisis stirred the feelings she'd been trying to dismiss. "I can still take Maddy, though."

Nodding, he glanced toward the kitchen. "Coffee?"

"Please." She adjusted Connor in her lap so his head rested against her chest while she caressed his hair.

"Here you go." Jake set her mug on the side table. He'd even added cream.

"Thank you."

Taking a seat on the stool opposite her, Jake stared into his own cup. "So…have you thought about what I said last night?"

Though Connor's fever might be on its way down, Alli felt her own cheeks heat. Sure, she'd anticipated that the topic of last night might come up, just not so quickly. "Yes, but—"

"Good morning!" Maddy bounded into the room, startling Alli. Jake, too, judging from the way he nearly spilled his coffee.

And bringing an end to their conversation. Something Alli was fine with, because the look on Jake's face gave away nothing to indicate if he'd changed his mind or still felt the same way. Although, the fact that he seemed eager to broach the topic gave her hope.

By the time Maddy finished her breakfast and got dressed, Jake had secured a nine-thirty appointment with the pediatrician in Brenham, leaving Alli a good thirty minutes to gather her thoughts before she and Maddy departed.

To Alli's delight, today's group for story hour was even larger than last week's. And just like last time, the kids were engaged, asking questions and fully experiencing the stories. Alli couldn't be happier.

After saying goodbye to the last of the families, Alli retrieved her phone, hoping to find a message from Jake regarding Connor's doctor visit. She wasn't disappointed.

Ear infection. Picking up antibiotic before heading home.

She noted the time stamp. Forty-five minutes ago. They were probably home by now. Or close, anyway.

"Can we get lunch?" Maddy peered up at her.

"Without your brother?"

"We could take him something."

"That's probably not a good idea since his tummy's upset."

"Daddy and Mimi give me soda when my tummy hurts. We could get Connor a soda so he can feel better."

Did the girl know how to drive a bargain or what? "Okay, I suppose we can stop."

Her phone rang as they pushed through the double doors at the front of the library into a bright, sunny day. Suspecting Jake, Alli retrieved the phone to see Tonya's name.

"Hello?"

"Alli?"

"Hey, Tonya."

A shaky breath came through the line. "Are you still at the library?"

"I'm just walking out now. What's up?"

"I don't suppose you could meet me at Whataburger so we could talk? Just for a few minutes."

Alli's thoughts immediately went to Connor. "I don't know. Maddy and I are about to pick up some lunch, but her brother is sick at home, so I probably need to get back."

"Oh." The disappointment in Tonya's voice wrenched Alli's heart.

"Tell you what. Let me see how he's doing, and I'll call you right back."

She ended the call and dialed Jake. "Hey, how's the patient?"

"Sleeping. Mom is with him now while I take care of some chores."

"I hate to ask, but Tonya wants me to meet her at Whataburger. She sounded kinda down. Would you mind if Maddy and I grabbed some lunch there? I promise to keep things brief."

"Not at all. Things are covered here."

Her shoulders sagged with relief. "Thank you, Jake."

"You're welcome. And hey."

"Yes?"

"Don't forget, we have a conversation to finish."

Her insides fluttered and her cheeks felt flushed. "I'll let you know when we're on our way."

While Maddy climbed into her booster seat, Alli texted Tonya to let her know they were headed to Whataburger, and a short time later they were walking into the fast-food restaurant. The aroma of grilled meat filled the dining area, awakening Alli's appetite as she scanned the space to see Tonya wave from a table in the corner.

Holding Maddy's hand, Alli gestured that they were going to place their order first, and Tonya acknowledged with a nod.

She smiled somewhat nervously when Alli and Maddy finally approached the table, armed with their drinks and the orange-and-white tent with their order number. "Thank you for meeting me."

"No problem." Alli set the drinks on the table.

"Miss Alli." Maddie patted her arm. "I need to go potty."

Alli cast a glance Tonya's way. "Sorry. I'll leave our number here in case they bring our food."

"Sure." The other woman nodded. "I'll be here when you get back."

Thankfully, their food was waiting when they returned several minutes later.

"Sorry about that." Alli took a long draw of her Diet Dr Pepper before helping Maddy unpack her grilled cheese sandwich. "So what's going on?" She glanced Tonya's way. "You sounded kind of down."

The woman shrugged. "Sometimes the memories just kind of sneak up on me, you know?"

Cup in hand, Alli offered a weak smile. "I understand." She took another swig of her soda. "Are you still seeing your counselor?"

"Not since I moved. The one I saw in Austin gave me a couple of names before I left, but I haven't contacted anyone yet."

Why hadn't Alli asked about that the first time she'd run into Tonya, when she mentioned she'd moved to Brenham? "Tonya, it's imperative you have some sort of support system in place. Are you still living with your aunt?"

The woman across from her nodded.

"Do y'all ever talk about Lacy?"

"Only if *I* bring her up. My aunt says she won't because she doesn't like to see me cry."

"Tonya, I want you to contact those support groups your previous counselor gave you."

"Yeah, I can do that." Her focus shifted to Maddy. "How's that sandwich?"

Was she purposely trying to change the subject? Or did she just not want Maddy to feel left out?

"It's yummy," Maddy said around her most recent bite.

Another long drag on her straw and Alli found herself sucking air. Drat. Sadly, she had a rule. No refills until she ate some protein.

"How come you don't have any food?" Maddy asked the woman across the table, who had only a large cup in front of her.

"Because I ate it all before you got here."

"Oh." Maddy picked up another French fry.

Meanwhile, Alli took a bite of her burger, trying to come up with some way to help Tonya, but she couldn't seem to focus. She felt…tired all of a sudden.

Obviously she needed more caffeine. "I need a re-fill." She reached for her cup, nearly toppling it. And when she tried to stand, the whole room began to spin.

"Alli?" Tonya was beside her now. "Are you okay?"

"Yeah—I—" She looked at the woman beside her, but it was as though she were looking through a tunnel.

"You don't look so good, Alli. Perhaps we should get you to a doctor."

"Maybe she's sick like my brother," Alli heard Maddy say.

"Maddy, pack up your food please. We need to get Miss Alli to her car."

Alli wasn't sure she could walk that far.

She felt an arm come around her. It had to be Tonya.

"Stay right with us, Maddy," Tonya said. "Hang on, Alli. I'm going to get you some help. Where are your keys?"

"Purse." At least Alli thought she said the word aloud. Right now the only thing she was sure of was that something was seriously wrong. She'd never felt this way before.

And as Tonya helped her into the passenger seat of her Jeep, Alli had just enough wherewithal to realize she'd been drugged. But how?

Her drink. She'd left it. Taken Maddy to the bathroom.

Had Tonya done something? Was she planning to take Maddy?

Alli couldn't let that happen. She'd promised to protect Jake's children.

She tried to scream, but darkness was closing in. *God, help! Protect...*

Jake aimed the utility vehicle toward the house just before three that afternoon, eager to check on his son.

Not to mention talk to Alli about last night. At least Connor's outcome was fairly predictable. After a couple doses of antibiotics and a good night's rest, he'd be as good as new. If only he could be that certain about the situation with Alli.

Watching that funnel cloud drop out of the sky yesterday had a wave of terror washing over Jake. Naturally, he feared for the well-being of his kids and Alli, but it was more than that. In the midst of his fear, it was as though a veil had been lifted, granting him a clarity he hadn't had in a long time.

He didn't just love Alli as a friend. He was falling *in* love with her. And he really hoped his kiss—make that kisses—had relayed just how deep his feelings for her ran. He wanted her in his life. Not just temporarily, but for always. And thanks to Tori's news about the learning center, Alli had one less reason to leave.

Of course, he still had to overcome her skepticism where he was concerned. The way he'd taken her for granted when they were teens shamed him now. Yes, she said she'd forgiven him. But last night proved she hadn't forgotten.

He wound the vehicle around a limb that'd been downed by the storm. Thankfully, his hay meadows hadn't suffered much damage from the hail and his herd was all accounted for. The windshield on his truck had a major crack, though, and would need to be replaced soon. Meanwhile, Alli's Wrangler only suffered a couple of minor dings.

As he neared the house, he was surprised to see his mother's vehicle still in the drive. And a second look revealed Alli's Jeep was nowhere to be found. He thought for sure she'd be back by now. Unless she'd already been there and gone. Still, it wasn't like her to leave this early. Not without letting him know.

His chest tightened. Was she afraid to face him? What if she didn't share the same kind of feelings he had for her? Then again, the intensity of her kiss had only been matched by his own. Or had he imagined that?

Man, he wished he'd been able to talk with her this morning. To find out where that "yes, but" was leading. Yes, but she needed more time. Yes, but she wasn't interested.

Pulling up to the house, he barely killed the engine before hopping off and hurrying inside. In the living room, his mother sat in the recliner with Connor in her lap, sucking those two fingers.

He smiled when Jake moved in front of them. Then leaned toward Jake, his arms outstretched.

Lifting the boy into his embrace, Jake said, "How you feelin', buddy?"

His son simply nodded.

"Have you heard from Alli?" His mother stood, concern in her creasing brow.

An unwelcome feeling settled into Jake's gut. "I was about to ask you the same thing."

"I tried calling her," his mother said, "but it went to voice mail. I can't imagine her lunch with a friend would last this long."

"Especially with Maddy." He tugged his own phone from his pocket and dialed Alli's number.

"Hi, this is Alli."

He ended the call without leaving a message. "It's not like her to go this long without checking in."

His mother nodded, her worry evident.

"I'm going to contact Bill." He scrolled through his

recent calls. "See if he's heard from her." He tapped Bill's name.

"Hey, Jake. What's up?"

"Have you heard from Alli?"

"Not since she left for your place this mornin'."

Hmm… "She made it over here." He explained about Connor and Alli saying she was going to meet Tonya at Whataburger. "She still isn't back. Mom and I have both tried calling, only to get her voice mail."

"That doesn't sound like Alli." Bill's voice lowered a notch. "'Specially since Maddy's with her."

An uneasy feeling settled in Jake's gut. "My thoughts exactly."

After a long pause, Bill said, "I hate to mention this after what you went through with Bethany, but you don't s'pose they could've been in an accident, do you?"

The fears Jake had been trying hard to ignore catapulted to the surface like a beach ball held under water. He passed Connor to his mother and stepped away, reliving the night he'd gotten the call about Bethany. And while his initial response had been very un-Christlike, he'd soon been overcome with a grief that was deeper than anything he'd ever imagined. Even more so than when his father died. Because not only had his children lost their mother, any hope he had of fighting for his marriage had died right along with Bethany.

He cleared his throat. "The thought crossed my mind."

"I think I'll go drive their route," said Bill. "See if I can find them. Maybe they had car trouble. You know how spotty cell service can be."

"While you do that, I'm going to give Brady James a call." Brady was an old friend of both Jake and Alli's who was a sheriff's deputy. "He should be able to find out if there've been any accidents."

"Call me back if you learn anything."

Less than sixty seconds later, Jake had Brady on the line. He laid out his concerns. "Can you check to see if they were involved in an accident? Because I can't come up with another reason why I wouldn't have heard from Alli."

"Let me check with Dispatch and I'll call you back."

Jake moved to the refrigerator and grabbed the tea, feeling helpless. And he didn't like it one bit. He retrieved his glass beside the sink. Added some ice. *God, I know You know where they are. Wherever that may be, I pray that You'll protect them. And please, lead me to them!*

As he poured the tea, his mother appeared in his periphery, still holding Connor.

"I know what you're thinking, Jake. You can't let yourself go there, though. You have to stay strong for Maddy. And for Alli."

He lifted the glass and took several gulps.

"You love her, don't you?"

Facing the woman who'd always been there for him, he said, "That obvious, huh?"

She nodded. "As much now as it was when you were in high school."

"Where Maddy, Awee?" Connor cocked his little head with all the innocence of a child.

Abandoning his tea, Jake took his son into his arms and held him tight. "They'll be back soon, bud." He prayed so, anyway.

A knock sounded at the door.

For a moment, Jake and his mother simply stared at each other. Then he passed Connor back to her, strode across the living room and yanked open the door to find Brady on the other side. And while panic threatened to get the best of Jake, he forced himself to take a breath.

"Good news," Brady said. "There've been no major traffic accidents in the area and none involving a Jeep Wrangler."

Jake exhaled slowly. "That's good. Though I still have no idea where Alli and my daughter are."

"Which is why I'm here." With a surreptitious nod, Brady urged Jake onto the porch.

Closing the door behind him, Jake asked, "What's going on?"

"When was the last time you heard from Alli?"

"A little before noon."

Nodding, Brady stroked his clean-shaven jaw for a moment before looking at Jake. "You said your son was not with them."

"No, he woke up sick."

"What's the relationship like between Maddy and Alli?"

Jake shrugged. "Great. Maddy adores her."

"Have the two of them ever gone off alone before?"

Jake's gaze narrowed. "No. Whatever you're getting at, Brady, I suggest you spit it out."

"Is it possible Alli could have kidnapped your daughter?"

"Aw, come on Brady. You know Alli. Why would you even think such a thing?"

"Because I'm a cop. You used to be one, too. You know how cases can take bizarre twists. Even with seemingly innocent people."

"Yeah, well, not with Alli. She was meeting a former client for lunch."

Brady straightened. "What sort of client?"

"Alli was a caseworker with CPS. Recently she ran into a woman she knew who'd lost her daughter."

"Lost her how?"

Jake explained the situation as succinctly as he could.

"And Alli stays in touch with this woman?"

"She happened to run into her in Brenham a while back. You know how kindhearted Alli is. She gave the woman her number and told her to call if she ever needed to talk."

"And has she called Alli?"

"Today was the first time that I'm aware of. Though Alli saw her at the Brenham library last week. Alli reads for their story hour. Tonya, I believe her name was, called her today and asked if they could meet for lunch. Alli checked in with me first, though, to make sure it was okay."

"And you haven't heard from her since?"

The sound of a vehicle coming up the drive at a fast rate of speed had Jake looking to see Bill's truck approaching.

"No." He moved to the edge of the porch. "Bill drove their route to see if maybe they'd had car trouble."

But when Bill got out of his truck, he shook his head as he headed their way. "Nothin' out of the ordinary." He joined them on the porch and shook Brady's hand.

Returning his attention to Jake, Brady said, "Did Alli happen to mention where she was meeting this other woman?"

"Whataburger." Jake straightened as instincts that had served him well on the streets of Houston began to kick in. "You think Tonya might have something to do with their disappearance?"

"Strong possibility."

Jake looked from his friend to Bill and back, the hairs on his neck lifting. "You might be right."

"Then I need you to tell me everything you know about this Tonya person."

Over the next hour, Jake and Bill shared every bit of information they could recall about the distraught woman. Which wasn't near as much as Jake would've hoped, but being the professional that she was, Alli had tried to protect the privacy of her cases.

Francie had joined them by the time Brady went to his vehicle to pass information on to his superiors, and Jake called his in-laws to make them aware of the situation and ask them to pray. He wasn't surprised when Ted said they were on their way.

Jake gathered his son, thankful his fever was gone, and stepped outside for some fresh air. Except for the trip to the doctor, the kid had been cooped up all day. He stood him beside the new swing set.

"Where Maddy?" The innocence on the boy's face as he looked up at him had Jake's insides twisting.

"With Miss Alli."

"I wan d'em come home." Connor's bottom lip pooched out.

Jake cleared the emotion lodged in his throat. He had to stay strong for his daughter. And the woman he cared so deeply for. *God, please help me.*

"Me, too, bud. Me, too."

The sound of boots on gravel had him turning to see Brady approach.

"A statewide Amber Alert is being issued," said the deputy. "And the sheriff is working on getting surveillance video from the restaurant. In the meantime, every officer in the area is on the lookout for Alli's Jeep, so I'm going to head back to the office."

"I'm going with you." Hands on his hips, Jake glared at Brady.

His friend smirked. "Given your background, I anticipated as much." He started for the door. "You'll have to take your own vehicle, though."

After bringing Connor back inside and repeating what Brady had told him to his mom and the Kreneks, Jake kissed his son goodbye and headed out the door. He prayed all the way to the sheriff's office, asking God to give him strength, both mentally and physically, and to lead the authorities to Alli and Maddy. And by the time he stepped out of his truck, he felt the same drive and mindset he'd had when he worked patrol in Houston. The kind that allowed him to manage situations with a calm and strength of character that could only come from God.

Inside, he asked for Brady, who escorted him into the offices just as someone said, "They found the vehicle."

Jake knew better than to get his hopes up. Just because they'd found the vehicle didn't mean Maddy and Alli were in it.

"It's at the Countryside Motel off Highway 290," the woman in her midforties said. "Officer spoke with the desk clerk, who did not recognize Miss Krenek. Though the little girl was with the woman who checked in."

That meant Maddy was okay. But what about Alli? Where was she?

He fisted his hands. *Lord God, help me hold it together. Keep a level head.*

"Get a team over there now." The sergeant eyed Brady. "That means you, James."

Jake stepped toward the sergeant. "Sir, I'd like to request permission to go with them. My little girl's life could be in danger."

The man, who was slightly shorter than Jake, stared up at him. "I understand your concern, but I can't allow that."

"I'm former HPD. I know procedure."

The sergeant's gaze narrowed. "Then you're aware what you're requesting isn't procedure."

Yeah, he knew. But he had to try. He couldn't just sit here, waiting. Wondering. "With all due respect, sir, this is my little girl we're talking about. I need to be there for her." And Alli.

The man appeared to relax a notch but didn't break eye contact. "If I were in your shoes, I'd be making the same request." He heaved a sigh. "You will be unarmed and will remain in the cruiser until the situation is secure. Do you understand?"

"Yes, sir."

Turning, the sergeant caught Brady's attention. "Get him a vest. Just in case."

Chapter Fourteen

Alli heard Maddy's soft giggle from somewhere in the distance. There was another voice, too. Kind of familiar, but she was having trouble distinguishing who it belonged to.

She tried to open her eyes, but they refused to cooperate. That was okay, though. She hadn't felt this relaxed in a long time. Maybe she'd just rest.

"When is Miss Alli going to wake up?" Maddy's question penetrated Alli's fog.

Was Maddy waiting on her? Alli shouldn't keep her waiting. If only she could muster the energy to get up.

"She's still not feeling well," the other voice came. "So we should let her rest," the woman continued. "Would you like me to read you another book?"

Who was reading to Maddy? And where was Connor? Alli hated for him to miss out.

"No, thank you."

Alli felt herself smile. Maddy was using her manners. She was such a good little girl.

"Can we go outside and play?" Maddy loved to play outside.

"Not right now, Lacy. We need to stay here and keep an eye on Alli."

"Who's Lacy?"

Maddy's question had Alli forcing her eyes open, though she seemed helpless to move anything else.

Her gaze darted around the space. There was a second bed opposite the one she lay on, with a deep-green-and-gold-geometric bedspread. A small, flat-screen television sat next to a microwave atop a chest of drawers at the foot of the bed. And in the corner to her right, beside a small, round table, a woman sat in a chair holding Maddy in her lap.

Alli squeezed her eyes shut, willing her brain to wake up. Opening them, she again looked at the woman with strawberry-blond hair.

Tonya Hayes? What was Lacy's mother doing here? How did they get here? Why couldn't Alli remember anything?

Panic welled inside her, though she did her best to suppress it for fear Tonya might realize she was awake. The woman wasn't in her right mind. And if she felt threatened, there was no telling what she might do. Including hurting Maddy.

While Tonya began another book, Alli lay still, trying to get her brain to work so she could figure out how to get out of here. Wherever here was. But it wasn't going to be easy when every extremity felt as though it had a hundred-pound weight attached to it, rendering her virtually immobile.

Tears welled in her eyes and trailed out the corners into her ears. She'd always hated that feeling.

God, I have no idea where we are. Help me find a way to get Maddy to safety. Please, please, protect her. I can't let anything happen to Jake's little girl.

She supposed it was too late for that, though. Somehow, Alli had allowed herself to be compromised, leaving Maddy in the hands of a woman who was obviously unstable. But then, who wouldn't be after trying to save your child, all the while fighting for your own life?

The thought had Alli trying to ward off another round of tears. She needed to stop them before Tonya realized she was awake. But how?

Alli lay still, willing her breathing to level out, trying hard to remember what had happened. How did they end up in what appeared to be a hotel room? Why was she so groggy? Had she been drugged? How could she have allowed something like that to happen?

So many questions, yet her mind seemed void of any answers.

Lord, I don't care what happens to me. Just, please, get Maddy back into her father's arms. Jake has already lost his wife. He can't lose his daughter, too.

My grace is sufficient for thee: for my strength is made perfect in weakness.

The verse from Second Corinthians rolled through her mind like movie credits. How she could remember that when she couldn't recall how she got here was a mystery. All she knew was that she'd never felt more helpless than she did right now.

God, I will trust in Your grace. You're all Maddy and I have right now. Help us.

Someone banged on the door.

"Sheriff!"

Alli felt her eyes widen. She knew that voice but couldn't put a face to it. She remained perfectly still, waiting to see what Tonya would do.

"I can get it." Maddy slid out of Tonya's lap.

"No, no! I'll get it." Standing, Tonya set Maddy back

in the chair. "Thank you for letting me read to you. Now you stay right here while I talk to the officer." With that, Tonya turned, walked to the door and opened it. "I only wanted some time with the little girl."

Two officers took hold of Tonya and escorted her outside while two more entered the room.

The first appeared to be searching for something and kept a hand on his weapon while the other approached Maddy and knelt to her level.

"Mr. Brady? Why are you here?"

That was the familiar voice.

"Well, I heard there might be a problem," he said. "Are you okay?"

"Mmm-hmm. But Miss Alli got sick. Ms. Tonya put her to bed so she could rest."

Brady briefly glanced Alli's way as Maddy continued.

"Then she read me lots of stories. And we ate fruit snacks and Cheetos. She even let me have soda."

"Well, I have some good news," said Brady. "Your daddy is right outside, and he can't wait to see you."

Jake was here?

Of course he was. Not only was he a doting father, he was a former police officer. This had to be tearing him apart.

Maddy hopped out of the chair. "Let's go see him."

A third officer entered. A female.

Brady addressed her. "Can you take Maddy to her father while I check on my friend over here?" He nodded toward the bed.

"Sure." The woman smiled and held out her hand. "Let's go find your daddy."

Alli breathed a sigh of relief. Maddy was safe, and Jake could rest easy now—while Alli's heart shattered into a million pieces. She'd promised to protect Jake's children and yet she'd endangered his little girl. Just like she had Lacy.

Thank You, God, for watching over Maddy and keeping her safe.

"All clear." The first officer emerged from what she assumed was the bathroom as Brady dropped beside the bed where she lay.

"Alli, are you hurt?" His blue eyes were filled with compassion. He'd always had the prettiest eyes.

"Don't...think...so." Getting the words out took a major effort. It was as though her mouth and brain were disconnected. "Hard." She swallowed. "To. Move."

Standing, he hollered, "We need medical care in here!"

After a once-over, the EMTs transferred her to a gurney and wheeled her out of the ground-level room surrounded by countless vehicles with flashing lights.

Fresh air filled her nostrils, and she took a deep breath, willing it to clear the cobwebs from her brain.

The sky was a midnight blue streaked with the slightest amount of gold in one direction, but whether the sun was setting or just coming up, Alli had no idea. She wasn't even sure *where* she was.

"Miss Alli!" Turning toward the sound of Maddy's voice, she saw the little girl pointing at her from the protection of her daddy's arms.

As he started toward her, Alli feared the disdain she was sure to see in his eyes. But his expression was guarded. Intense as he motioned for the EMTs to stop. How had he found them?

Then again, he was a former police officer. More than that, though, he was a father who would move mountains to find his precious child.

Maddy peered down at her. "I'm sorry you got sick." She awkwardly brushed her blond curls away from her face. "But I'm glad you finally waked up."

"Me. Too." Even Alli's smile felt strange.

Jake stared at her, lines creasing his brow, his gaze a steely gray. "Alli—"

"Jake, we need you over here!" Brady hollered somewhere behind her.

Jake nodded in that direction, before looking at Alli again. "I called your dad. He'll meet you at the hospital."

She simply nodded as tears threatened. Of course he'd called her father. Jake had Maddy to take care of. And he probably wouldn't let her out of his sight for a very long time.

His shoulders seemed to sag as he continued to stare at her. "I know they want to talk to Maddy, but I need to talk to you. And I'm going to see to it that happens just as quickly as possible, okay?"

He was probably going to shred her for putting Maddy in danger. And Alli couldn't really blame him. So once again, she nodded.

A tear streaked down her cheek as he walked away. And while she wouldn't have thought it possible, her broken heart shattered a little more.

The EMTs continued toward the ambulance, and as they backed her inside, she glimpsed a police SUV across the way. Or more importantly, the woman in the back seat.

Alli could only imagine the charges that would be brought against Tonya. Sadly, prison wasn't what she needed. She needed help to overcome the tragedy she'd lived through and still carried with her every day. And while true healing could only be found in Jesus, Alli was going to do everything she could to get Tonya the emotional help and support she needed because there was no way Alli would allow Lacy's father to claim another victim.

Jake approached Bill's front door shortly after eleven the next morning. Bill had texted him around ten, letting him know Alli was home and resting comfortably. So with Connor back to his old self, Maddy oblivious to the danger surrounding yesterday's events, and Ted, Brenda and Jake's mother happy to dote on both kids, Jake took the opportunity to slip away.

He was thankful Alli's father had his back because all of Jake's calls to Alli had gone straight to voice mail. And though he'd tried to tell himself her phone might be dead or turned off, or that she was asleep, it had done little to console him. At least now he'd be able to see her, hold her, tell her how much he loved her.

He had to force himself to breathe as his mind drifted back to yesterday. When he saw them wheeling Alli out of that motel room, he'd feared the worst. It felt as though his heart had been ripped out of his chest. And while the glazed look in her eyes assured him she'd been drugged and, effectively, rendered defenseless, he was thankful she was alive.

Yet for as much as he'd wanted to stay with her, to comfort her, hold her close and never let her go, the authorities needed to question Maddy, leaving him no choice but to remain with her. He'd never been so torn.

Now he knocked on the door and waited. But before it opened, the sound of tires on gravel had him turning to find a sheriff's SUV pulling into the drive. Brady emerged as Francie opened the door.

"Hey, Jake." She poked her head outside and smiled Brady's way.

"Good timing," said the deputy as he approached. "Now I can talk to everyone at the same time."

Jake felt his brow lift. "Sounds like you've got some information."

Brady looked at Francie. "Mind if we come inside?"

Jake had to tamp down his desire to whisk past both of them and find Alli. But he didn't have to wait long.

Bill stood from his seat on the hearth as they entered the family room. "Come on in, fellas."

Alli was stretched out on a recliner beside the fireplace, wearing yoga pants, a sweatshirt and socks, her hair around her shoulders. She was the most beautiful sight Jake had ever seen.

He continued toward her and dropped a kiss on her forehead. "How are you feeling?"

Her expression guarded, she simply nodded.

Taking hold of her hand, Jake assumed Bill's spot on the hearth beside her. "Brady says he wants to talk to us."

Four pairs of eyes fixed on the deputy as he eased onto the sofa.

He looked at all of them before focusing on Alli. "The lab report showed Rohypnol in your system." He scanned the faces watching him. "Often referred to as the date-rape drug. It's a sedative that can also cause some amnesia."

Jake felt Alli's grip tighten as Brady continued.

"Surveillance video in and around the Whataburger showed Alli placing two drinks on the table and conversing with the suspect before disappearing for approximately six minutes. During that time, the suspect is seen adding something to the larger of those two drinks.

A short time later, Alli is seen returning to that table, consuming the beverage that had been tampered with, and soon becoming seemingly disoriented or intoxicated. The suspect then helped Alli into a Jeep Wrangler registered in Alli's name. Maddy is seen entering the back seat of the same vehicle before the suspect gets behind the wheel and drives away."

Again, Brady looked from face to face. "Surveillance cameras at the motel were disabled. However, the desk clerk was able to ID Mrs. Hayes as the person who requested the room and confirm that Maddy was with her when she did so."

Alli pulled her hand from Jake's to rub her forehead. "I can't believe I don't remember any of that."

"Memory loss is indicative of the drug you were given." Brady stood. "It may take you a couple of days to bounce back, so take it easy."

Looking up at him, she said, "What's going to happen to Tonya?"

He sighed. "She's facing some serious charges. Not the least of which is kidnapping."

Alli slowly nodded. "I understand. I'd just like to see her get the help she needs." Looking at Brady again, she continued. "Thank you, for all your help. Dad told me how you picked up on the offhanded comment that I met with Tonya and set things in motion."

"You never know when a hunch might pay off." He pointed to Jake. "This guy here knew something was wrong when you weren't back in a reasonable amount of time. But then, once a cop, always a cop."

"And aren't we thankful for that," said Francie. "We owe you both a big debt of gratitude."

"Just doing my job. Now I'm going to get out of

y'all's hair." Brady turned for the door, but Francie stood to stop him.

"Not without some cookies, you don't."

After Brady left, Bill and Francie made themselves scarce, leaving Jake alone with Alli. Something he was more than a little grateful for.

Hands clasped tightly in her lap, Alli kept her gaze fixed on them. "How is Maddy?"

"Fine. To listen to her tell it, yesterday was simply an adventure. Tonya told her you weren't feeling well and needed to rest while they read books and ate junk food." He dipped his head, hoping to coax her into looking at him. "In other words, she was oblivious to any danger."

"But she *was* in danger." She looked at him now. "Who knows what could've happened? I promised you I would protect your children. And I failed."

He stared at her. "Alli, I don't believe that for one minute. Yeah, you promised to do everything in your power to keep my children safe. And you did just that for as long as you could. Until you were rendered powerless. Then it was up to God. Believe it or not, there are things that happen in this world that we have no control over. We just have to trust that God has our back. That no matter how bad a situation might seem, He's still there. So you may think you were putting my daughter in danger, but I know God was with you every moment, watching over you and Maddy, protecting you."

She glared at him. "You cannot tell me you weren't worried."

"Not as much as you'd think. Until I saw you wheeled out on that gurney. And I realized that if something had happened, I might never get the opportunity to tell you how much I love you."

She looked away. Cleared her throat.

He reached for her hand. "I mean it, Alli. I love you."

When she finally turned toward him again, her face was unreadable. "Should you choose to keep me on, I will continue to watch Maddy and Connor until your mother returns from her trip. Then I will be leaving Hope Crossing."

His gaze searched hers, looking for some indication she was joking. "Of course I want to keep you on. Not only because of the kids, but because I love—why would you do that? Just walk away?"

"Because I want what's best for all of you. And it's not me."

"Where are you going?"

"I don't know, but teaching is no longer a part of my plans."

"Why not?"

"I've let down two little girls who depended on me to protect them. I can't afford to disappoint any more children. Now, if you would please leave, I need to rest."

He couldn't believe this was happening. Didn't want to believe it. He dragged a hand through his hair. It had to be the drugs talking. She'd see things more clearly once they were out of her system. Wouldn't she?

He could only pray.

Straightening, he looked down at her. He never thought he'd see the day, but Alli had lost her fight. And it was tearing him apart.

"Why don't you wait until Monday to come back? Give yourself a few days to recuperate. If you need more time, just let me know. But there's one thing I don't want you to forget, and that is that I love you. And that's not going to change."

With that, he turned and left.

Chapter Fifteen

Alli awoke Friday morning, glad to be back in her garage apartment. Her dad and Francie had doted on her the last two days and taken good care of her, but she needed her own space again. Because, while her body was feeling more like its old self, her heart still ached. For Maddy, for Jake, for Tonya. And for herself.

There was a time when she used to dream of hearing Jake Walker say he loved her. Now that he had, she couldn't accept it. Not because she didn't want to or didn't reciprocate his feelings. On the contrary, it was her love for him and his children that had her turning him away and deciding to leave Hope Crossing so they could move past the drama she'd brought into their lives and go back to the carefree bucolic lifestyle they'd enjoyed before she showed up.

Okay, she supposed that was rather theatrical, but she'd rather live somewhere else, knowing Jake and his children were safe, than with them, fearful her choices might cause them harm. She could only pray the next few weeks with them would be uneventful.

She supposed she was going to need that time, though, to determine where she wanted to go and what she was going to do with her life. Children had always been a driving factor in her decisions before, but she couldn't afford that anymore. Perhaps there was something somewhere she could do behind the scenes that would still benefit children. However, at the moment, she didn't have the slightest idea what that might be. Maybe she'd do some research after breakfast.

Stepping outside, she breathed in the morning air. Not too humid and just the right temperature. Perfect weather for Maddy and Connor to enjoy their new swing set.

Her steps slowed as she neared the bottom of the stairs. She couldn't love Jake's children more if they were her very own. Though over the last couple of days, she'd realized that her feelings for the two of them paled in comparison to what she felt for their father.

Shaking off the morose mood, she continued to the house, noting that Francie's vehicle wasn't in the drive. And since Dad was probably somewhere around the ranch, it looked like Alli would have the house to herself. Just as well. They'd been treating her with kid gloves ever since she came home from the hospital.

The aroma of bacon awakened her appetite as soon as she walked in the door. She continued into the kitchen, hoping Francie had made some biscuits to go with it.

"Hey there, Alli Cat. I was wondering when I'd see you."

She nearly jumped out of her skin. Whirling to face her father at the table, she pressed a hand to her chest. "Daddy, you scared me. I thought you were gone."

"Nope. Been waitin' on you." Standing, he moved toward her for a hug. "Didn't mean to startle you. Sorry 'bout that."

She savored the embrace. "Where's Francie?"

Releasing her, he said, "She and Gloriana are heading into Houston to shop for baby furniture. Why don't you grab some coffee while I git you a couple of biscuits and some bacon."

She smiled up at the man she'd always adored. "Only if I can pour you another cup, too."

"You got it."

Minutes later, she'd made herself comfortable at the table and was savoring her first sip of the steaming liquid when her father set a plate in front of her. "Thank you."

"You're welcome." He settled into the chair next to hers, watching as she split one of the biscuits in half and spread butter on it before adding a slice of bacon she broke in half.

She took a bite.

Holding on to his mug, her father said, "I've been thinking about this notion of yours to run off to somewhere unknown and give up on your plans to become a teacher. Kinda sounds to me like you're running away."

Her chewing slowed and the small bite felt like a boulder going down.

She took another sip of her coffee. "Between what happened to Lacy Hayes and the kidnapping the other day, I don't trust myself to care for children anymore."

Moving his drink aside, he clasped his hands on the table and stared at her. "Need I remind you that *you* were the one who fought to keep Lacy in foster care. And nobody could've foreseen an innocent lunch at Whataburger turning into a kidnapping." He sighed. "Besides, you can't run away from your problems, baby girl. No matter where you go, more will always find you."

Tears pricked her eyes, but she blinked them away.

"Do you remember that time Jake's horse bucked you off?"

"It's been mentioned a time or two in recent weeks." She sniffed. It was only by the grace of God that filly hadn't crushed her skull.

"Do you remember how heartsick Jake was?"

Nodding, she picked at her second biscuit. "He was ready to have Mazie put down until I talked him out of it."

"It broke that boy's heart, thinking he'd put you in a position where you could've been injured a whole lot worse than you were."

She puffed out a chuckle. "Aside from doing my chores, he insisted on carrying my backpack when I went back to school."

"'Cause he blamed himself for what happened. Kind of like you're doing now."

Finally, she looked him in the eye. "This is different, Daddy. There's no telling what could've happened to Maddy."

"But it didn't."

"What if things had turned out differently?"

"Hmm, like what if you'd allowed Jake to apologize all those years ago?"

With a huff, she crossed her arms. "You're playing dirty now."

"Am I?" He rested his elbows on the table. "Baby girl, do you realize how many blessings I'da missed out on if I'd allowed what-ifs to dictate my life?" Reaching across the table, he cupped her chin and urged her to look at him. "You've always been a strong, independent woman of faith. And your faith has carried you through some tough times. What makes this any different?"

Her chin began to quiver, and she pulled away. "I've

never felt so helpless. There was nothing I could do to help Maddy."

"You know what your mama always used to say. *Your weakness is the perfect canvas—*"

"*For God to display His strength.*" She'd said those very words to Jake the night of the fish fry when he was feeling like a failure.

Daddy leaned back in his chair. "You know, when we danced at the wedding, you suggested you were incapable of loving. I don't think that's the case at all. I think the problem is that you gave your heart away a long time ago and never bothered to get it back."

He was right. Her heart had always belonged to Jake.

She nodded, tears spilling onto her cheeks as she recalled the pained look in Jake's eyes the day she'd told him she was leaving.

Her father handed her a napkin.

Taking hold, she blew her nose. "Before Jake left the other day, he said he loved me."

Daddy's brow furrowed. "Then would you mind telling me why you're still sittin' here? Get on upstairs and fix your face and go tell that boy you love him, too. Good night, nurse, he's been through enough without you breakin' his heart, too."

She couldn't help the laugh that puffed out. "When you put it that way…" She didn't want to cause Jake any more pain.

She hugged her father tight, feeling more hopeful than she had in a long time. "Thank you, Daddy."

On her way upstairs, she retrieved her phone from her pocket and pulled up Tori's number. Since it was a school day, Alli sent her a text.

I'd like to apply for that director position. Send me details when you have time.

Back in her apartment, she changed clothes and primped in record time before heading back downstairs to her Jeep, which had been returned yesterday. Her heart raced and her stomach fluttered as she backed out of the drive and headed toward Jake's.

God, the only thing I'm certain of right now is that Jake loves me, and I love him. Everything else, my future, is in Your hands, and I firmly believe Your grace is sufficient.

She couldn't seem to get to Jake's fast enough. Hard to believe that only an hour ago, she was running from him. Now she was racing toward him.

Rolling up his drive minutes later, she saw the kids playing on their swing set. Jake was pushing Maddy in her swing while Joanna propelled Connor in his. Their movements slowed when they saw her Jeep. And when she finally came to a stop, both children hurried to greet her.

She got out of her vehicle, promptly kneeling to embrace both of them. "I missed you two so much."

"We missed you, too." Maddy released her and took a step back. "Do you feel better?"

"I do, thank you." Still holding Connor, she stood to meet Jake's curious gaze. "I feel better than I have in a very long time."

"Alli, darlin'." Joanna moved in for her own hug. "'Thank you' doesn't begin to convey my gratitude. I'm proud of you." Releasing her hold, she met Alli's tearful gaze. "I love you so much. You're like the daughter I never had."

"You were always like a second mother to me."

When her eyes finally cleared, she saw Jake standing a few feet away, his arms crossed, his face unreadable.

Standing Connor on the ground, she looked from him to his sister. "Why don't the two of you go back to swinging while I talk to your daddy." Her gaze shifted to Joanna. "Would you mind?"

Jake's mother waved her off. "Not at all. You two take as long as you need."

As they made their way back to the swing set, Alli crossed to where Jake stood, her heart pounding wildly. "Mind if we go around back?"

He didn't say a word, simply motioned for her to take the lead.

Nearing the garden that now boasted vegetables ready to be harvested, she stopped and waited for Jake to join her. Instead, he kept a good two feet between them. Just out of her reach, the way she'd always thought him to be.

She swallowed hard, her gaze darting from him to the grass and back. Then, with a deep breath, she said, "I love you. And I need to know if you still love me."

He tilted his head. "Surely you don't think my love for you is something I can just turn off."

She felt like a tongue-tied teen. "I'm going to stay in Hope Crossing."

He lowered his arms. "For how long?"

She shrugged. "I was kinda thinking forever."

His slow smile told her he was pleased. Finally, he eased toward her. "When we were kids, you always said you wanted six children. Do you still feel that way?"

"It would be nice. At my age, though, it might be a little challenging."

"Since when is Alli Krenek not up for a challenge? Besides, we've already got a head start with two." He stopped in front of her, setting a calloused palm against her cheek.

She stared into his eyes, feeling like she was finally home for good. "Just what are you saying?"

"That I can't wait for you to be my wife. Alli Krenek, will you marry me?"

"I thought you'd never ask." Pushing up on her toes, she pressed her lips to his, allowing herself to give and receive love for the first time. Nothing had ever felt better.

When they finally parted, she said, "I do foresee one problem, though."

Worry puckered his brow.

"Where will we put all those babies?" She shrugged. "Your house only has three bedrooms."

His smile grew wide. "That's easy. It's a two-story house. We'll just finish out the upstairs."

"A man with a plan." She caressed his cheek. "I like it."

He tugged her closer. "And I love you."

Epilogue

The late October air had Alli shivering as she locked the door of the Hope Crossing Early Learning Center shortly after six on Friday evening. And to think, most of the kids had worn shorts today. Now, thanks to a cold front that had arrived earlier than expected, it was suddenly jacket weather. Making this the perfect night for a bonfire.

"I cowd, Mama." Standing next to his sister, now-three-year-old Connor hugged himself.

Alli smiled at the pair, feeling beyond blessed as she took hold of each of their hands. "Come on, let's get to the Jeep."

She and Jake had married at the end of June, giving them a few weeks to settle into their new life together before Alli started her position as director of the learning center. A position she was enjoying more than she'd expected. Being a part of building something new and exciting had invigorated and challenged her. And the larger teaching staff had allowed them to accommodate even more students, including Maddy and Connor.

"We gots to hurry, Mama." Inside the vehicle, Maddy buckled her seat belt.

While they were running a few minutes behind thanks to a late-arriving parent, Alli assured Maddy, "We'll be fine. Daddy's got everything ready, so all we have to do is change clothes."

Alli had been looking forward to tonight all week. An opportunity to kick back and relax with family. Hawkins and Annalise, who recently announced they were expecting another child, had invited them to a chili supper at the tree farm. Gloriana and her family, which now included three-month-old Benjamin, would be there, too, along with Francie and Daddy. Joanna would've been included if it wasn't for the fact that she was on another cruise. This one out of Galveston was her second this year. She and Ginny had enjoyed themselves so much in Alaska, they were planning at least a half dozen trips over the next couple of years.

In addition to supper and the bonfire, Kyleigh was going to oversee pumpkin painting for the kids. Something Maddy had been talking about all week.

Yet as Alli started her Jeep, she found her own excitement building, making her every bit as eager as Maddy to get there.

Jake had already loaded the camp chairs and blankets into the truck by the time they arrived at the ranch, so he helped the kids change while Alli pondered her own attire. And less than fifteen minutes later, they were on their way to the tree farm. The Hope Crossing Christmas Tree Farm, to be exact. A place that a month from now would be bustling with folks in search of the perfect Christmas tree. Including Alli. She looked forward to building all sorts of memories with her new family.

Though the weather had turned cool, it wasn't windy, making a bowl of chili around a crackling fire one of those simple pleasures. Especially with her husband beside her.

"I'm going to get seconds. Can I get you anything else?" Jake leaned toward her until their shoulders met, the reflection of the flames dancing in his eyes. "Chili? Chips? Cornbread?"

"How about a small sliver of cornbread?"

He smiled. "It'll cost a kiss."

Her own smile widened. "And here I thought you were simply being nice." She pressed her lips to his.

With a wink, he said, "I'll be right back."

As he walked away, she knew she'd finally found someone besides her father to call her hero. Jake was her best friend, biggest supporter and the best partner she could've asked for. He made her feel more than loved. He made her feel treasured.

He was also turning out to be a pretty good carpenter. Now that they'd decided on a layout for the upstairs of their house, he'd finally begun the framing process. And that was a good thing.

Watching sparks drift into the night sky, she was filled with so many memories of doing this same thing as kids. These same families hanging out, relaxing after a long week to catch up with one another. Back then, she never would've dreamed of living anywhere else but the country. Thankfully, God had led her back home. And granted her the desires of her heart, too.

"Who wants to paint a pumpkin?" Kyleigh announced after everyone had finished eating.

Maddy's was the first hand in the air. "I do."

"Me, too," said Connor.

"Me!" Little Olivia grinned.

"Okay, follow me." Kyleigh herded them toward the barn where light spilled from the open door.

On the opposite side of the fire, Gloriana bounced baby Benjamin, who'd been a tad fussy. "Come on, buddy. Give me a burp."

Itching to get her hands on him, Alli stood and approached her friend. "May I hold him?"

"Absolutely." Gloriana handed her the blanket-wrapped bundle.

No sooner had Alli set him to her shoulder and patted his bottom a couple times than the infant let out a belch far too big for someone so tiny.

As Gloriana returned to her seat, she glanced up at Alli. "Show-off."

Still holding the babe, Alli returned to her own chair and simply stared at him, her heart swelling with anticipation.

Jake leaned toward her, moving the blanket just enough so he could get a better look at the little fellow. "They sure do grow fast. Doesn't seem that long ago Maddy and Connor were that size." He glanced at Alli. "Who knows? Maybe one of these days they'll have another brother or sister."

Alli couldn't help the grin that spread across her face. "Yeah. Maybe sooner than you think." She simply watched her husband then, waiting to see if he picked up on what she was subtly trying to convey. She hadn't been to the doctor yet, but she'd done three home tests this week, and every one of them had a positive result.

She heard a slight gasp from the other three women gathered around the fire, but they promptly clamped their mouths shut.

Meanwhile, Alli stared at her clueless husband.

"That would be nice, wouldn't it?" He looked from the baby to her. "I can't wait."

While this wasn't how she'd planned to tell him—

not that she really had a plan—she couldn't help herself now.

"Good. Because I'm pregnant."

His smiling face morphed into confusion before his goofy grin returned, bigger than ever. "You're? Really? You're not messing with me?"

Gloriana approached. "I think this might be a good time for me to retrieve Benjamin."

Alli handed her the baby, her gaze never leaving her husband's. "Near as I can tell, we're going to be needing that upstairs space sometime in June."

While her husband continued to gawk at her, her father said, "Jake, if you don't hurry up and hug her, I'm gonna beat you to it."

"We're gonna have a baby." Jake said the words slowly, as if he was still trying to convince himself. "We're gonna have a baby!" Standing, he pulled Alli to her feet and wrapped an arm around her, cupping her face with his other hand. "Believe it or not, round about that time I asked you out back in high school, I used to dream of something like this one day playing out."

"No way."

He nodded slowly. "Yes, way."

Caressing her lips with his thumb, he continued, "That means you've made two of my dreams come true."

She felt her brow pucker. "What was the other one?"

"You agreeing to marry me." He kissed her then, and Alli knew she was right where she belonged. In the arms of the only man who'd ever held her heart.

* * * * *

If you enjoyed this Hope Crossing story, pick up the previous books in Mindy Obenhaus's miniseries:

The Cowgirl's Redemption
A Christmas Bargain

Available now from Love Inspired!

Dear Reader,

Whether this is your first or third visit to Hope Crossing, I'm so glad you stopped by. Grab a kolache or some Blue Bell and let's chat a bit.

I don't know about you, but I get excited when two people who belong together finally overcome space, time and/or obstacles to find their happily-ever-after. Of course, sometimes overcoming those things is what strengthens their relationship, making it even more special.

Jake and Alli made themselves at home in my head over a decade ago. But it never seemed to be the right time to tell their story. Until now. And I loved watching these two finally come together.

Like Alli, sometimes we're our own worst enemy. We allow fear to keep us from going after what we really want instead of recognizing what God has put right in front of us. Indeed, fear can be a powerful thing. But God is bigger than our fears, and His grace is sufficient to help us overcome them, if we'll just let Him.

I hope you enjoyed this journey to Hope Crossing and pray you'll visit again. Book four in the series will be out just in time for Christmas. Until then, I would love to hear from you. You can contact me via my website, mindyobenhaus.com, or find me on Facebook—just search for *Mindy Obenhaus, author*. And don't forget to sign up for my newsletter so you'll be in the know about new releases and giveaways.

Until next time,
Mindy

COMING NEXT MONTH FROM
Love Inspired

THEIR ROAD TO REDEMPTION
by Patrice Lewis
Leaving his shameful past behind, Thomas Kemp joins a newly formed Amish community in Montana. It's not long before he meets young widow Emma Fisher and her toddler daughter. Their bond could mean the family that Thomas has always wanted—but can he keep his past from ruining their future?

A CONVENIENT AMISH BRIDE
by Lucy Bayer
Grieving widower David Weiss has no plans of finding love again, but when local woman Ruby Kaufmann offers comfort to his daughter, they agree to a marriage of convenience. They both decide to keep their hearts out of the arrangement, but it isn't long before that promise starts to unravel...

THE NURSE'S HOMECOMING
True North Springs • by Allie Pleiter
After ending her engagement, Bridget Nicholson returns home to figure out the rest of her life. So she takes on a job as Camp True North Springs' temporary nurse. The last thing she expects is to find old love Carson Todd also working there. Will it derail her plans, or could he be what she's been searching for all along?

A COWBOY FOR THE SUMMER
Shepherd's Creek • by Danica Favorite
All that stands between Isaac Johnston and running his own camp is an internship with rival Abigail Shepherd at her family's horse farm. The problem is, he's terrified of horses. Can Abigail help Isaac overcome his fears and prove there is more to them—and her—than meets the eye?

THE BABY SECRET
by Gabrielle Meyer
Arriving a few days early to her sister's wedding, Emma Holt hopes to relax after a tragic end to her marriage. When she meets best man Clay Foster and his baby daughter, things start to look up—until she discovers a secret about his baby that could tear them apart...

THE WIDOW'S CHOICE
by Lorraine Beatty
Widow Eden Sinclair wants nothing to do with her bad boy brother-in-law, Blake Sinclair. When he comes home unexpectedly, she fears the shock will be too much for his ill father to handle. Then she discovers why Blake really came back. It might threaten her family—and her heart as well.

LOOK FOR THESE AND OTHER LOVE INSPIRED BOOKS WHEREVER BOOKS ARE SOLD, INCLUDING MOST BOOKSTORES, SUPERMARKETS, DISCOUNT STORES AND DRUGSTORES.

LICNM0523

Get 3 FREE REWARDS!

We'll send you 2 FREE Books **plus** a FREE Mystery Gift.

FREE Value Over **$20**

Both the **Love Inspired®** and **Love Inspired® Suspense** series feature compelling novels filled with inspirational romance, faith, forgiveness and hope.

YES! Please send me 2 FREE novels from the Love Inspired or Love Inspired Suspense series and my FREE gift (gift is worth about $10 retail). After receiving them, if I don't wish to receive any more books, I can return the shipping statement marked "cancel." If I don't cancel, I will receive 6 brand-new Love Inspired Larger-Print books or Love Inspired Suspense Larger-Print books every month and be billed just $6.49 each in the U.S. or $6.74 each in Canada. That is a savings of at least 16% off the cover price. It's quite a bargain! Shipping and handling is just 50¢ per book in the U.S. and $1.25 per book in Canada.* I understand that accepting the 2 free books and gift places me under no obligation to buy anything. I can always return a shipment and cancel at any time by calling the number below. The free books and gift are mine to keep no matter what I decide.

Choose one: ☐ **Love Inspired Larger-Print** (122/322 BPA GRPA) ☐ **Love Inspired Suspense Larger-Print** (107/307 BPA GRPA) ☐ **Or Try Both!** (122/322 & 107/307 BPA GRRP)

Name (please print)

Address   Apt. #

City   State/Province   Zip/Postal Code

Email: Please check this box ☐ if you would like to receive newsletters and promotional emails from Harlequin Enterprises ULC and its affiliates. You can unsubscribe anytime.

Mail to the **Harlequin Reader Service:**
IN U.S.A.: P.O. Box 1341, Buffalo, NY 14240-8531
IN CANADA: P.O. Box 603, Fort Erie, Ontario L2A 5X3

Want to try 2 free books from another series! Call 1-800-873-8635 or visit www.ReaderService.com.

---

*Terms and prices subject to change without notice. Prices do not include sales taxes, which will be charged (if applicable) based on your state or country of residence. Canadian residents will be charged applicable taxes. Offer not valid in Quebec. This offer is limited to one order per household. Books received may not be as shown. Not valid for current subscribers to the Love Inspired or Love Inspired Suspense series. All orders subject to approval. Credit or debit balances in a customer's account(s) may be offset by any other outstanding balance owed by or to the customer. Please allow 4 to 6 weeks for delivery. Offer available while quantities last.

Your Privacy—Your information is being collected by Harlequin Enterprises ULC, operating as Harlequin Reader Service. For a complete summary of the information we collect, how we use this information and to whom it is disclosed, please visit our privacy notice located at corporate.harlequin.com/privacy-notice. From time to time we may also exchange your personal information with reputable third parties. If you wish to opt out of this sharing of your personal information, please visit readerservice.com/consumerchoice or call 1-800-873-8635. **Notice to California Residents**—Under California law, you have specific rights to control and access your data. For more information on these rights and how to exercise them, visit corporate.harlequin.com/california-privacy.

LIRLIS23

HARLEQUIN
PLUS

Try the best multimedia subscription service for romance readers like you!

Read, Watch and Play.

Experience the easiest way to get the romance content you crave.

Start your **FREE TRIAL** at
<u>www.harlequinplus.com/freetrial</u>.

HARPLUS0123